A NEW WAR (LP)

VOL. 1 THE ERRANT

JACK R. STANLEY

WRIGHTBRIDGE PRESS

To the love of my life,
Mary Lee,
who makes all things possible.

A New War
Vol. 1 THE ERRANT
Copyright © 2021 by Jack R. Stanley.
All rights reserved.

Edited by
Mary Lee Stanley
and
Rose Marie Reed
ISBN: 978-1-954212-01-5
Wrightbridge Press

jacks@wrightbridgepress.com
www.thefictionwritersnotebook.com
www.jackrstanley.com

[Murder in Muleshoe]
If you were murdered would they try to find the killer or plan him a parade?
[Guns Along The Rio]
In 1858, two fresh-off-the-ranch 17-year-olds join the Texas Rangers. What could possibly go wrong?
GO TO: eepurl.com/dKEi_Y

CHAPTER ONE

A former Hudson-Sturdivant T-rex class battleship known as "Flying Terror" raced in from behind a gas giant. It flew in and then started backwards, keeping station one click off the bow of the grand passenger cruiser, THE STARDUST. The T-Rex was the most massive of types of battleship used in the Corporate Wars.

The predatory ship fired seven precisely placed rockets, disabling the pleasure craft's communications arrays. Simultaneously, the red banner with a white skull and black left eye patch with crossed sabers behind it was beamed to every monitor screen onboard from the bridge to the casinos. This was the pirate symbol of

Bartholomew Lutz — the unquestioned pirate sovereign. Over the bridge speakers came the command, "Come to a complete halt, or there will be no survivors!"

The order wasn't repeated. It didn't have to be. The cruiser's skipper, Captain Jilson Merriman, 50, knew who he was facing. Still, he had to project calm if any were to live. Had the pirate flag been black no one aboard would be left alive.

Two smaller warships uncloaked to the port and starboard sides of THE STARDUST -- one a corvette and the other a frigate — each former property of different corporation space navies.

The classy, tall, and clipped bearded Captain knew what was ahead. He also grasped the fact that there was absolutely nothing to be done about it.

"This is THE BLACK DEATH! Open your outer airlocks! Stand by to be boarded," a penetrating voice of the pirate captain said. It was Bartholomew Lutz, and the commander of the passenger ship knew it was the voice of death.

To his bridge crew, Captain Merriman calmly said, "Open outer airlocks." Flipping a switch, he addressed the entire ship. "This is the Captain speaking. Stay where you are. Do not lock any doors. We are being boarded by pirates. Anything beyond what I have instructed will only make it worse on you and those around you. As per United Corporation rules, we are unarmed and defenseless."

Within minutes, umbilicals from the ships on either side of THE STARDUST attached to the open airlocks and teams of pirates stormed aboard. They split to preassigned destinations. A gang of five entered the bridge with handheld blasters. Their leader, a woman in a tight red EVA (Extra Vehicle Activity) suit and bubble helmet, blue squiggles painted on her face, killed Captain Merriman with a shot to his heart. The rest of the woman's team, also clad in EVA suits, did the same to the rest of THE STARDUST's crewmembers. The pirates then disabled the ship's locator, scrambled its ID code, and took command of the vessel.

Other pirates raced down corridors and blasted open any locked doors. They did not wear EVA suits but coveralls and pieces of different corporate disc-o-lite. Each was unique in color and cut. They were an unkempt lot, the men in various stages of facial and hair growth. The women displayed cleavage and tattoos.

On sight, these savages murdered the older passengers, anyone they considered sixty-five or above in age and began sorting everyone else. Five to thirty-five-year-old males and females were herded into the largest of the vessel's dining room. These were destined for the sex slave markets. Infants too young to care for themselves were killed instantly.

The rest of the passengers, entertainers, and crew were jammed into the auditorium. This lot was bound for the open slave market and whatever tasks their new owners desired, from house cleaning to farming, to mining.

Both captive groups were ordered to strip and pile their clothing in the center of the dining room or on the auditorium stage, respectively.

Seventeen-year-old Jaxlynn Shellanberger, a cute girl about to turn eighteen in two days, was on this trip with her family to celebrate her birthday. A six-year-old toe-headed boy was frozen in fear. Once Jaxlynn had rid herself of her clothes, she noticed the shivering child and helped him undress. He cried, and she took him in her arms as he wrapped his shaking legs and arms around her and tried to bury his face in her neck.

When all the hostages were naked, the pirates fired glitter bombs that showered the prisoners. Green was used for the sex slaves and red for the others. The powder and flakes clung to the victim's skin. Each tiny piece was drug-coated. Within half a minute, all the captives were catatonic and pliable. Jaxlynn eased the child she had tried to protect to the floor beside her. He did not resist and stood beside her silently.

The pirates were disciplined and efficient in their jobs. This was not their first raid. No molesting was attempted because they all knew the virgins of both sexes would bring the best prices and market, which translated into more credits for each pirate.

From his bridge, pirate Captain Bartholomew Lutz watched screens of multiple bodcams from his crew. The short chested attack commander smiled a cruel grin displaying his mouth of gold teeth. He had a gold nose ring in his left nostril and three sapphires in the cartilage of each ear.

A separate team took their time blowing open each safe from the steward's office to individual staterooms. Cash and valuables were gathered from the shipboard stores, casinos, and payment stations across the ship.

It took over three hours to sort the human cattle and to clean out the coffers.

The bodies of dead crew and passengers were spaced through the nearest airlock. The raider's work continued even as the now unnamed vessel followed the other ships into the empty dark of space toward their undiscovered port.

THE STARDUST would never be seen or heard of again. It became one of the missing and mystery ships of the galaxy. The captives would likewise vanish into lives of short rations and interminable days of wretched existence until they died. A select few would join the pirate ranks and become what they had recently feared the most. These would have depraved lives of excess and brutality. The only winner would be Bartholomew Lutz.

CHAPTER TWO

The free-for-all erupted into a full riot in a lower section space station bar. The shaft thin proprietor laid his blunderbuss-looking riot stunner across the bar pointed toward the middle of the fight.

"Hold up there," said an average-sized man, having just entered the establishment. He had a dirty blonde ponytail at the back of his bald head and wore a floor-length brown robe with the hood thrown back. He could be a healthy 60 or, given the current state of genetics, 120. From his pocket, he produced a leather pouch. The newcomer slid the modest sac up the bar to the owner. "I'll cover the damages."

The barkeep lowered his weapon and checked

the contents. He took one coin from the sac and bit on it. The shiny metal gave way slightly, proving it was pure gold. Satisfied, the owner shrugged and put his stunner back under the bar.

Across the room, a big man with shoulder length, thick russet hair took the smashing from a plastisteel chair right across his back. Neither the chair nor the man bent or broke. In fact, the man didn't even flinch. He was 6' 2, all muscle with a ragged but matching reddish-brown beard covering the bottom half of his face. At the moment, he was lifting a stout little fellow over his head like a full keg of whiskey. Then the redhead tossed his victim across three tables and into the wall. Next, his deep green eyes sought the chair thrower. He dropped that solidly built but equally muscular attacker with a fist full into the face.

Before the current conflict broke out, the establishment was only barely serviceable for its rough clientele. Even then, it could have been mistaken for a human rat hole. Thus the reason the saloon could only find a location on one of the bottom-most rungs of the space station.

"This a private fight?" the man in the robe asked, stepping into the combat zone and speaking to the distracted big man. "Or can anybody join in?"

The brawl's center figure only glanced at the new arrival, who might be mistaken for a member of some Druid or some other religious order.

"You a miner?" the big man asked, fending off two other toughs — one with a kick to the chest and the second with an elbow in the ear.

"I've handled my share of laser picks and concussion hammers."

"You union?"

"Freeborn, independent, and plan to stay that way."

"Then welcome," the larger man whipped around and aimed his head as a weapon at the newest participant, intending it to be a headbutt.

But the smaller opponent sidestepped and ducked to avoid the move, almost as if he had been expecting it.

"Thanks," the robed man said as he grabbed the shaggy man's back collar, now that he was bent at the waist. The cloaked man snapped up a knee that connected with the clavicle bone of the attacker. The lead combatant landed groaning in pain — down on his butt.

This surprised the big man who forced himself back to his feet facing the newly invited member of the party. The big man got to his feet, stepped back, drew a massive fist that he held as he cocked his head. Then his expression changed.

"Doc?" he asked.

"Top of the morning to you, Ash!" The newest member of the melee nodded to the big miner.

"What the hell are you doin' here?"

"Looking for you, my friend," the robed man said before planting the toe of his gravity boot in the big man's right thigh.

Ash reacted to this surgically placed strike, and his right knee almost buckled.

"Ouch!"

"Had enough?" Doc asked, returning to a defensive stance. "We could go get a drink in a decent bar."

"I don't drink anymore, Doc."

"Then what are you doing in here?"

"Enjoying their local sparkling water. Recycled of course. I don't recommend it."

Doc smiled and said, "Then I may have a proposition for you."

Ash rubbed his leg, trying to decide.

"Or we can keep on fighting," the monk character said as he smiled.

"Okay," the big man said. "You've got me."

Grabbing his duffle from its resting place at

the bottom of a support post, Ash asked, "How did you find me?"

"I didn't. Clell's been working on it for a while."

The big man understood his friend was referring to his personal AI. Everybody had one. These implanted microdots lived below the external occipital ridge at the back of the skull where the spinal column's ligaments attached. Designed to be personal and private, audible only to the host. The implants were infinitely upgradable at different stages of life. Members of the military could access the Communication Web, where one can find anything and almost anyone in the multiverse. But they were untraceable unless the owner had switched his locator on.

"You are one hard son-of-a-bitch to locate since the war," Doc said.

"Didn't know anybody was looking for me. I wasn't looking for anybody. I kind of wanted solitude."

"No, you didn't. I'm sure you thought you did, but I've figured you out, Ash. And being a loner ain't it."

"Oh, I can't wait to hear this," Ash said with as much sarcasm as he could muster. He opened his duffle and fished out his leather poke. He extracted a single crystal the size of an acorn and tossed it to the barkeep. Despite fending off flying debris from the fight, the man caught the nugget.

"Here," Ash announced while the quartz was still in the air. "This is to cover the damage."

"I already had that covered," Doc said.

The proprietor caught the dull angled glass. "This disc-o-lite?"

"Should be enough to cover the damages," Ash said, stowing his small bag and slinging the duffle over his shoulder.

"If this is real, it's enough to buy half the commercial spaces on this ring," he said, putting the stone under an authenticating light mounted beneath the under edge of the bar to help detect counterfeit currency and ore samples.

"Just make sure you rebuild this place," Ash, the big man, said. "Miners need a good place to drink and fight. You can keep the change."

"Done," the barkeep grinned. He tossed the sack of gold coins back to the monk. "Hey, who started this?"

Ash shrugged and said, "I did. It's my birthday."

Out in a corridor, Ash asked, "What's with the Obi-Wan Kenobi get-up?"

Instead of answering, Doc said, "You're awfully free with your money."

"It's just money. There's more where that came from. What the hell else would I do with it?"

"Save it?"

"For what?"

"A nice condo — a custom-built house — maybe a vineyard."

"And do what, sit and rust for a hundred years or two?"

"Ash, there will always be another war. Plato said the only ones who are beyond knowing that are the dead."

"And look where Plato is now."

Doc smiled as they stepped outside to the walkway. The windows along the wrap-around corridor looked out on the darkness of space and the dots of light, distant stars, galaxies, and other worlds.

"What have you figured out about me?" Ash said as they walked.

"First of all, just because you are an orphan that does not make you a loner. You, my friend, are a guy who needs family."

"Doesn't the orphan part kind of cancel out the prospects of a family?"

"Not at all. Family isn't blood. Your crew has been your family."

"And I got over half of them killed."

"Before any of that you thought Lella was — or could be — the beginning of the family you wanted. That is why you married her, but she never was — as much as you wanted it. I'm here to help you find a new family. A family without betrayal."

CHAPTER THREE

They moved up two levels and found seats in a bright-colored restaurant. Ash had to check his duffel with the bot at the entrance, but he took his poke with him. Their table looked out on the sprinkled light of thousands of stars.

Doc scratched the bald center of his head and pulled his darkly streaked blond ponytail out of the back of his robe before sitting.

"So have you come to terms with Lella?"

"Don't you think it's about time, Doc?"

"I thought that a good year after she was killed," Doc said. "But it had to be on your schedule. Everybody deals with grief and…."

"Complicated situations?"

"That's a good way to put it."

Ash asked, "You mean the way she died or what she was?"

"Both, I guess — although the out-of-control drone was supposed to make it look like an accident."

"Supposed to?"

Ash's beautiful wife of a half-dozen years had died when a fully loaded cross-continental cargo delivery drone suffered a significant malfunction shortly after takeoff. The craft slammed into the 157th floor of a two hundred story luxury apartment, killing Lella and the man she was having an affair with at the time. The crash started a multi-story fire on that floor. The inferno took nineteen more lives before the auto fire suppression system and firefighters doused the flames.

Doc took a deep breath and let it out before he said the hard part.

"What if I told you that cargo drone that killed Lella and all the others — was a pirate craft? It had more fuel onboard than it needed. It was a continental not an international flight — and it was on an assassination mission."

"For who?"

"The man Lella was with — and her."

"Why Lella?"

"They were afraid she might know too much. Pillow talk spills lots of beans."

Ash chewed on this a moment.

"Doc, Lella was a sex addict. I understand that now. And I've learned to deal with it — I think."

"You think?"

"Lella was who she was. And I was who I was. I should have seen it in one of us before we got married. The signs were there. I was an addictive personality and so was she. Yes, she made a fool out of me — but given time, I might very well have done the same to her.

"My deployments were exactly what she needed in a husband. And what I needed to cover my drinking. When I was home — and when we sent comms to each other — she flawlessly played the devoted wife — I the professional husband. I never questioned her when she said she couldn't have a kid. Truth is, she didn't want them. I don't think I did either. They would have gotten in the way — of the parts both of us were playing."

"And if someone today mentioned that she was a — slut — let's say — how are you going to react?"

"Doc, everything she was was part of the woman I married. What I've learned about her — condition — I'm not sure she had a choice to be what she was. Or why I was blind to it — unless one addict knows another or unknowingly keeps the secret. Part of it had to be my fault. From what I know about — her addiction — and mine — it never made either of us happy. It was like a carrot on a stick — but never within our grasp. Still we both allowed it to happen."

"Are you telling me you're not bitter?" Doc asked.

"About her or about the sailors I sent to their deaths? I hope I've gotten over both — or at least as much as I can. It's past — there's not a damn thing I can do to alter either. I live with it or — let it eat me up little by little. I think I've moved on."

"I must say, I'm amazed."

Ash chewed on this information a full minute.

"You sure about this, Doc? Lella's death?"

"It's official — at least the facts are — but its information the corporations don't want to get out. It's much better written off as a horrible accident."

"And who is behind this?"

"Bartholomew Lutz. The pirate king."

The two men sat in silence for a while before Doc leaned forward once more and spoke.

"How about yourself, Ash? What conclusions have you come to? Surely you don't see yourself as a miner. You are a warrior. Military school — academy. You're also a good man — and a leader of men."

"Military school, as an orphan, was a lucky draw. Dillard Cosgrove pulled my name out of a hat. It surprised me as much as anyone."

"And the academy?"

"A logical next step. So was my service in Cosgrove's Corporation Forces. I'm also a fool and a jackass. A world controlled by corporations — who ever thought that would be a good idea. I also have no real perception of what women are. I can't even trust myself in that department."

"Betrayal is really what you're afraid of, my friend. Corporations don't give a damn. Bottom line is all they care about. And yet what you crave the most is a family."

"That your bottom line analysis of me?" Ash asked.

"I have a doctorate in both psychiatry and psychology. And trust me, betrayal is very common in human relationships. It's also the most harmful of maladies."

"Sorry, but neither your degrees nor your diagnosis helps much."

"I never expected they would," Doc nodded. "But I was hoping you had dealt with all that by now. It's your other qualities that have brought me here looking for you."

"Is there another war the corporation wants me for?"

"Not at the moment. There will be, of course."

"Always, Doc."

"And there'll be a need for someone like you?"

"I won't fight for the Corporation again — not Cosgrove — not any corporation. They rifted me all the way out to a civilian but kept me in the reserves. Thinking, I'm sure they could use me again in the next war. Wrong. I'm done with that."

"You're still a veteran."

"Doesn't mean a damn thing these days."

"Well, it means a little. There's free transportation. Not much of a perk, I'll grant you — but it's something."

A waiter arrived and the two friends ordered. "Wine?" the waiter asked before leaving.

"The best you have," Doc said. "He's paying," he said motioning toward Ash.

"No, I'm not. You came looking for me. This is on your tab." And to the waiter Ash said, "Green tea for me."

"Very good, gentlemen. I'll be right back."

"You were saying, Doc?"

CHAPTER FOUR

"You've done a lot of thinking in the last couple of years, my friend," Doc said, slowly turning his wine glass on the tabletop after they'd finished eating. "Sounds to me like you're getting lonely out on that asteroid. Just you with your AI to talk to. Sorry, but that sounds depressing as hell to me."

"Zulli rarely speaks unless spoken to. I like that. And she's developed a sense of humor — twisted and sarcastic as hell — but I like it.

"Thanks, my lord and master," Zulli said in Ash's head. Zulli was the name Ash had given his AI.

"And mining is a living," Ash continued to his friend across the table.

"Is it? Is it fulfilling?"

"I'm not looking for fulfilling or meaningful. Just one breath at a time."

"So you really are sober."

"I was yesterday, I am today — so far — but it's early. And I plan to be tomorrow."

"One day at a time?"

"That's the way it works. The best thing I can say about it is that I no longer have to worry about the corporation wanting me back. Not with my record."

"You are an award winning Captain."

"And a drunk. At least as far as they're concerned. The Corporation thought they'd bought and paid for me with all the genetic and other upgrades they provided. They didn't. I've paid them back all they're going to get during the war. I've fixed Zulli so they can never find me through her. Not even here right now."

The two friends sat in silence again for a few minutes before Doc said, "Disc-o-lite? You found disc-o-lite?"

"The company I bought the claim from thought it was mostly platinum — maybe a little nickel. Neither is worth what they once were. I think their drone fly-by was too quick. I took the time to check it out on the ground. To them it's just an asteroid like so many out here. Turned out to be more — only they didn't know it. They somehow screwed up their report."

Doc said, "You've always been one lucky son-of-a-bitch."

Ash shook his bushy head and smiled. "Is there a war somewhere? Is that why you came looking for me?"

"There is evil in the multiverse, Ash. And all it needs to triumph is for good men to do nothing. We are good men — good men with skills."

Ash didn't deny Doc's words.

A moment passed and then Doc said, "First, tell me — about your poke there — and your savings account. Maybe I can make this a sweeter deal. I assume you don't spend much."

"I don't need much."

"Well, how'd you like to be part owner of a re-furbished cruiser class merchant hauler? A Crux Chrysopsis carrier?"

"Crux Corporation Chrysopsis carrier? The smallest of their fleet carriers? It had what, fifty-two Scorpions fighters plus a shuttle?"

"Fifty-three. There wasn't but one on board when I found her. It and a shuttle were deadlined for parts. And of course, all the rest had been flown off-ship, and every life pod had been ejected, too. And those cruisers were big sons of a bitches. Even by military standards — but I thought that hanger space would make great cargo storage. I've also been able to acquire five retired Scorpions. They're fully restored and as dangerous as ever. The whole carrier is still fully armed and is both amazingly fast FTL and now cloaking capable."

"Somebody finally figured out cloaking?"

"And you won't believe the FTL improvement."

"We're still talking about a Crux Chrysopsis carrier?"

"We are. THE EASTERN CIRCLE they called her. Her old FTL drive redlined and burned a hole all the way through 10 decks and her outer hull. The captain expected her impulse engines to detonate. They didn't. He'd already ordered 'Abandon ship.' I came across her three years after the fact. Dead, derelict, and drifting. She's collided with a few asteroids, is my guess. She had damaged her locator beyond repair. I claimed her as salvage. I used what little impulse power I could get out of her to limp into the Xanadu Transit shipyards. That's off of Luna Ninteen in the Tatius solar system, Matheus quadrant of our Kermerus galaxy. It took me three years to even get there. Lucky for me, there was plenty of food on board."

"And now?" Ash was sitting forward, his big elbows on the table, his water between his arms.

"I happened to know the yardmaster at Xanadu Transit."

"Of course you do." Ash didn't doubt Doc's connections in the least.

"He owed me a few favors."

"Doesn't everyone?"

"It's the way the multiverse works, my boy. You scratch my back, and someday I'll scratch some itch you have?"

"Go on."

"Business is still a little slow there. Just getting started. A relative new station. It's growing, but slow. Anyway — we — the shipyard master and yours truly — own THE ERRANT together."

"THE ERRANT. Are you thinking of doing noble deeds?"

"At least good things. THE ERRANT's what we've rechristened her because I have high — and I guess noble expectations. She's registered and officially stamped approved. She's armed and fighting capable — but disguised as a merchant hauler. Oh, nobody but us knows she is still armed. To look at her, you'd think she was just a converted old carrier. But don't screw with her. She still has her teeth — only they're hidden. Even replaced her FTL drive with a much better one. And they have added a few improvements to her armaments."

"And cloaking?"

"Not only that, it even works while under way — in motion. We've made it a hell of a ship."

"Who is 'we'?"

"At the moment it's Santana Vanderhoof, Shipyard Master, and yours truly."

"A company?"

"We were sitting around trying to come up with a name when I noticed we were sitting at a small round table. So, to go with THE ERRANT, I came up with Round Table Ventures."

"You've got one ship and you're not afraid of the whole pirate fleet?"

"I wasn't a corporate marine, Ash. But I'm not afraid of anyone or anything. Now Lutz, and his ilk, have made some kind of deal with the corporations. They're pretty much picking on the small guys."

"Where do I come in? And why would I be interested?"

CHAPTER FIVE

"I was thinking of you as THE ERRANT's Captain," Doc said, sitting back in his brown robes. "But if you have the credits I expect you do, you could take over a third of her and be both Captain and part-owner."

"Nobody wants a drunk for a captain of a ship like that."

"We do — today — but it's early."

"And you?" Ash asked, taking another sip of his green tea. They were in a plush restaurant that looked out on a field of stars and the emptiness of space.

"I'm the ship's doctor — I was a real physician back when the profession still existed. These days it means I supervise and repair the autodocs —

plus manage the occasional surgical bot proce-
dure. But mostly, I'm the cook."

"Where did that come from?"

"There are many things about me you don't
know, Ash."

"I can't begin to imagine."

"Got a culinary degree during the three years
it took to get to Lima Ninteen. Still keep up my
skills. Are you interested?"

Ash didn't respond at first. "Tell me about this
war — and the crew you've got."

"You can pick the crew. A dozen can handle
everything if you have to — but I'm thinking
about a two hundred man expanded combat
company. That plus Scorpion pilots and maintenance crews. Could be up to five hundred plus."

"Doc, your idea is this surgical Paladin outfit?
Or are you thinking Robin Hood — obviously
you'd be friar Tuck?" Ash gestured to Doc's
attire?

"What I have in mind, my friend, is not a merc
force — well, okay, it is — but, let's call it a private military force. We pick our own fights. Even
if they're personal."

"So this is 'Have Space Navy — Will Travel.'"

"Kind of."

"Who would hire such an outfit? The corporations still have their tiny militaries — and Lutz does not harass their shipping. Well, only once in a while. Nothing that can't be written off. But —." Doc smiled, holding up several fingers, "the independents — and some colonies don't have the luxury of any kind of protection. They can't afford it — alone. But when they band together," he closed his fingers together, " — well, let's say our price will be right."

"You've thought this through."

"Three years on your own gives one plenty of time to cook and think."

"So, Bartholomew Lutz. I could get onboard with that. Who else?"

"There's another fight to be had in the Delporte quadrant."

"That's the other end of our quite sizable spiral galaxy."

"That's right. And it'll have to wait."

"For the moment you want to ride in and save the day for some not-so-big merchant."

"Even a colony or two on this end of the galaxy? And more like sneak in and murder their asses if they don't surrender — wipe out every operation. If and when we capture some of their ships — we can enlarge our own fleet."

After thinking to himself for a full two minutes and draining his cup, Ash finally said, "What the hell. I'm getting bored with mining, anyway."

The two men shook hands, Ash Kennett's massive grip dwarfing Doc Bywater's, but the older man shook with strength and purpose. They struck the deal.

"It'll take me a week or so to sell the claim and wrap up my life here."

"Fine. Meet me at Luna Nineteen's Xanadu Transit."

THE TWO MEN were waiting for Doc's transport back to the shipyards in the Tatius system.

"There's a troop transport headed to Seafort on the 28th," Doc told Ash. "They still take vets if they have space — and they always do. Transfer at Seafort, and I'll meet you a Lima Ninteen in a couple of months."

"I think I can do that." After a quiet moment between the two, Ash asked, "What about you, Doc? You're a religious scholar, too, right? You look like a monk — or a *Jedi warrior,*" Ash said with a wink. "Which are you — doctor, cook, or warrior?"

"All, I'd say."

"Really?"

"Always have been a religious scholar — to some degree."

"And all those girls in all the houses of delight and pleasure planets you've frequented?"

"Even the best of us fall off the wagon every now and then. Nothing better to land on than a pretty woman. And, besides, religion, faith, and celibacy don't always go hand in hand. There are some faiths where debauchery and sex itself is a blessed way of life."

"No doubt, you studied those ways in great detail."

"What's the point of scholarship if you don't truly delve into it?"

Ash couldn't help but chuckle.

"Another reason for these robes is that they allow me to carry nine weapons on me right now — none of which are detectable by any scanner. Just in case."

"I want to know about this other war you mentioned."

"It's on a modest planet called Camlann in the Delporte Quadrant."

"I've never heard of it."

"Few have. Camlann was discovered and inhabited over a thousand years ago."

Ash whistled. "At the other end of the galaxy — a hell of a long way out there."

"And not on any shipping lanes. There's nothing near it, so none of the corporations were or are even interested. That's the way the founders wanted it."

"And why are we interested in it?"

"There are two factions. The Fench and the Volles. Most of the present descendents on both sides are from the original escapees from pirate captivity. The rest were shipwrecked and lost — pioneers lucky enough to find this insignificant speck out where there's nothing else. Today, the Fench want peace and justice. The Volles want it to be wide open — almost a pirate haven — but there are no pirates there. And the Volles fight dirty."

"Doesn't everybody?"

"Not the Fench. They have long-forgotten notions of honor."

Ash studied his old friend for a moment before he went on. "And we'd be fighting for the Fench?"

"If they will take us. They're very clannish."

"Then, why should they? And why do we care?"

"You, my boy, are Fench. So am I. Camlann is

your home planet. You were born there. And today isn't your birthday."

"I didn't know that." Ash realized his mouth was open. "I've searched the records, and so has Zulli. There are none. Nobody knows where I came from. How would you?"

"I was there when you were born."

This caught Ash entirely off guard. "Then you know who my parents were?"

"I do, but that's a story for another day. Right now, the important thing is that you're a warrior — and a leader. Both are what the Fench need. In point of fact, they need you. They, like you, don't know it yet." After a pause, Doc added, "It's the destiny you were born to." Doc let that swirl around Ash's head a minute before he said, "There will be time for me to tell you all about it. After we finish off Bartholomew Lutz."

"Right. So it's Lutz first — and that won't be a quick or easy fights. Then it's the Camlann and the Fench."

Ash knew how mysterious Doc could be — but experience had taught him that the old man, who barely looked to be middle-aged, had thought all this through thoroughly. And, Ash trusted Doc.

"But you still owe me a conversation about who my parents were."

"Plenty of time for that while we're in transit. It takes five years to get to Camlann, even at FTL. We might have to sleep in stasis — wake and work in shifts. There will be time for me to tell you about your history."

"Then don't get yourself killed while we're dealing with the local scum."

"Oh, I don't plan to."

"No one ever does."

"By the way, a shave and a haircut would be a good thing for a Captain to have."

Ash ran an enormous hand through his beard and up to his shaggy head. "I think you're right, Doc."

CHAPTER SIX

All the life needs were discovered on a planet named Deadwood. It had a dominant, sufficient magnetic field, an ozone layer, an atmosphere, water, gravity, temperature, soil, and volcanic activity. When it was discovered, the Lancet Corporation believed they had an almost limitless source of silver. Thus the name from the old west bonanza mining town. The corporation invested quickly and lavishly in satellites and other infrastructure. This included a geostationary docking space station and planet first town, Butte, named after the gold strike town in Montana.

However, before the Corporate War began, the Lancet Corporation crashed into bankruptcy.

The supposed rich silver strikes turned out to be nothing more than the remains of heavy silver asteroids, which had struck the planet in its past. The deposits were numerous around the globe but they were scattered and shallow.

Deadwood was abandoned when the corporation went belly up, and its CEO committed suicide. There were no funds to retrieve the docking station and little interest in this, the sixth planet around a dying sun on the galaxy's outer edge. It was far from being a convenience for fright or trade.

One of the minor administrators on the then derelict space station was Bartholomew Lutz. Out of a job, he found a place with the Hudson-Sturdivant corporation. He showed a knack for organization as a supply agent. Even after he was militarized for service during the war, his natural abilities served him well. When the fighting abruptly ended, he pulled together like-minded men and women, and they turned pirate. Lutz engineered the theft of a T-rex battleship, which he renamed THE BLACK DEATH.

After killing the locator and ID transmitters, Lutz steered his prize to Deadwood. They docked and used shuttles to get to the planet's surface. Lutz changed the town name from Butte to Butt.

The pirates found farmers who had remained by choice or were left behind for suspected criminal activity. Lutz's organizational skills helped him build this pirate haven where might made right, and everything was for sale.

From his original crew, Lutz was able to find displaced and disgruntled members of the different militaries, which had been a part of the Corporate War. Most eagerly joined the cause of the skull and crossed sabers.

In the early years, every vessel under any flag was his target. He built his brotherhood of criminals, prostitutes, and murderous sailors and soldiers. They captured dry-docked corvettes and frigates from different corporation's stockpiles. They kidnapped the engineering and shipyard types needed. Lutz treated his abducted captives well if they showed a willingness to work for him.

A few corporations approached Lutz with offers of tribute to leave their planets, asteroids, and vessels alone. Never one to take the difficult path over the effortless but still profitable one, the pirate accepted the offer and sought out others. At first reluctant, even those companies who were reluctant came to heel when Lutz focused his attention on their assets.

With most corporations willing to pay generously to be left alone, the pirates had to turn their blood lust toward independent businesses. They developed the flourishing slave trade. The galaxy was rife with small corporations needing labor and individuals wanting pleasure slaves. Bartholomew Lutz was eager to fill these needs in exchange for credits, drugs, and even life staples.

Deadwood was a forgotten planet. Remembered by any who even knew the name, Deadwood was renowned as a colossal financial blunder. It was too far out to interest the most exploratory of corporations.

Pirates returning from a mission approached their home from the dark side of its third moon and stealthily came planet side to exchange goods and captives for instant payment in pre-washed and untraceable funds from the pirate bank.

Lutz kept passive satellites far out to detect any passers-by or the would-be approachers. The overwhelming majority of the detections were asteroids and comets. Others who drifted or for any reason looked in that corner of the galaxy were met with crushing force and disappeared.

The pirate world felt secure in its isolation and anonymity.

The captives from THE STARDUST were

marketed and shipped off planet after Bartholomew Lutz had his pick, the Butt brothels were restocked, and the planet's farm labor's needs were met. Now eighteen-year-old Jaxlynn Shellanberger was selected for Lutz's personal harem. The boy she had comforted during the first moments of her ship's raid, she never saw again.

THE LAST FIGHT of the Corporation Wars was called Zulu Thunder. It wasn't the name of a place but the tactical plan of the Cosgrove Naval and Marine forces. The campaign took place on an airless, unnamed and unnumbered moon.

The larger Crux forces fought the Cosgrove forces above the satellite to a standoff. This left the fate of the conflict, as it many times did, to the ground units. Here, too, Cosgrove was out numbered by 200,000 fighters. The only chance the Cosgrove Corporation had was in a subterfuge.

The second day of the battle the Cosgrove marines split into three groups. The Crux forces drove the most formidable remaining Cosgrove unit into a rocky valley where they took many casualties. The over confident Crux fighters swept into the valley, forcing the Cosgrove toward the box end of a canyon.

Making their last stand, the Cosgrove Marines held off the Crux forces until the rain of mortars and rockets crashed down from both sides of the valley. The supposedly straggling and disoriented Cosgrove troops from the 2 broken units had in fact hauled their heavier equipment into predetermined positions. When the signal was given, they ignited a deadly tempest. The door to the valley was closed behind the Crux forces and the trapped Cosgrove Marines exploded with a devastating hail of death which stopped the Crux advance cold. There, those believing they were soon to be the victors found themselves unable to escape the hell of destruction poured on them.

The surviving Crux Marines numbered less than a hundred.

The Cosgrove ships had slipped into positions where they decimated the Crux vessel down to less than a dozen before their admiral surrendered to a mere Cosgrove Captain. It was a humiliating defeat and quickly led to the end of hostilities across the galaxy.

CHAPTER SEVEN

Ash got passage aboard THE WINDY CITY a Wyatt Corporation general cargo ship. Ex-corporate military used the benefit of steerage space passage aboard regularly scheduled military transports. Regardless of corporation affiliation or previous rank, former military traveled from planet to planet, even system to system. Since the Reduction In Force (RIF.), the known galaxies were full of former corporation military after the war. Mostly they drifted from one destination to another. The Corporation Wars had bred a generation of former fighters who didn't fit in and couldn't easily hold a civilian job anywhere for very long. The passage of a dozen or more former soldiers, sailors, or marines on every troop mover didn't cost the corporations enough on their ledger to warrant its decimal point calculation with that many zeros in front of it.

There's a smell about any military installation, outpost, vehicle, or vessel, which Ash noticed the moment he stepped on board. It was a familiar and welcome mix of cleaning solutions, lubricants, and humans living in close quarters.

With a close-cut beard and modest haircut, Ash now looked like a redheaded Captain Nemo. He took a top bunk of a mostly empty billet bay and climbed the ladder to the number one rack above three others. He spent his days either reading from his playing card-sized flex tablet and working out in one of the open hanger bays. Mats covered the deck, and several cordoned off rinks awaited bouts. One could also choose to use racks of weights and lifting benches.

A week into the voyage, just as he finished his workout and wiped himself off with his towel, a young woman stepped up wearing tight shorts and a tank top. She looked to be in her early to mid-30s, but with genetics, there was no way of telling. She snapped to attention and spoke.

"Captain Kennett," she said with an abrupt military style.

Ash looked down at her and said, "It's simply 'mister' these days."

"Not to me, Sir," she said, holding her salute and fit body in her stance of respect. "When I heard you were aboard, Sir, I wanted to meet you and shake your hand if you wouldn't mind."

"We serve together?" Ash asked.

"Yes, Sir. Zulu Thunder."

Ash recalled the fight.

"We lost 22,000 in that pointless war."

"That we did, Sir. Many brave and courageous men and women. I was only a ground pounder," the young woman explained. "Twenty-second Marines of the 807th."

Ash returned her salute. "It was your outfit that turned the tide," Ash said, remembering. "Suckered the Crux battalion into a crossfire trap where you damn near wiped them out."

"Yes, Sir," she said. "But it was your plan. We just executed it."

"And almost everyone on our company took at least one hit. You wounded?"

"Twice, Sir. Lost my left arm — took a year to regrow it. But it was worth it."

Ash extended his hand to the soldier who stood as tall as her 5 feet seven inches would allow. She had a hard rock grip.

"I'm honored," Ash told her.

"The honor is mine, Sir."

"At ease. Where are you bound?"

She relaxed. "Not sure, Sir. Another security gig, if I can find one. I'm trying to get ahead of my reputation. They said I don't play well with others?"

"Civilians?"

"Usually. But I even have trouble with some vets who have lost their edge and never gave a damn about discipline in the first place. When I put in for a charge of detail, I expect a lot. Many out there will slide by doing as little as possible."

She had light brown hair and a hint of freckles across her nose. Her eyes were nut brown, and her other features were all attractive. But there was a decisiveness and directness about her which Ash knew put off casual friendliness.

"What's your name?" Ash asked.

"Perry, Sir. Birgitta Perry. They call me 'the Briquet.'"

"I'll bet they do," Ash smiled, thinking this came from her no-nonsense demeanor.

Corporate Space Marines had over a century ago adopted the naval rank structure. Senior non-com ranks which would have been a Warrant Officer under the new system. Ash preferred the old designations. Although an abbreviated form was generally used, Perry's official title would have been Senior Master Chief Petty Officer. It was a rank equal to the old army Sergeant Major.

"Senior Master Chief, it is an honor and a pleasure to meet you," Ash said, offering his hand again. He knew these were the toughest of the tough. "You're right, we've never spoken, but I know you well You were the N.C.O. for the company that baited the trap."

"Attack and Repel," she clarified her unit's mission, standing with her hands clasped behind her back.

"I came to see you while you were first in autodoc. You were in an induced coma."

"They told me, Sir." The woman smiled.

"What are your plans for the day?" Ash inquired.

"Lunch — or what passes for lunch on this bucket — then a swim, a run, and another workout this evening. Are you available for chow, Sir?"

"I'd be happy to share their S.O.S.," meaning chipped beef on toast or, in military jargon, 'shit on a shingle.' At 12:45, Master Chief."

"It would be my honor, Sir."

"Where's your dining assignment?"

"Starboard Amidships. Deck 41."

"S.A. 41," Ash said.

"Aye, aye, Sir."

"I'll see you then," Ash nodded and turned to go.

"Sir. I'd like to bring another shipmate of those days if you're amenable?"

"Any friend of yours, Master Chief."

CHAPTER EIGHT

Ash had guessed right about the fare being served — S.O.S. He met the young woman outside the hatch to the mess hall. Beside her was a scar-faced man who looked to be in his 40s.

The man, muscled and mustached, just short of six feet tall, had a staunch grip, which he and Ash exchanged after the man snapped to attention. Ash remembered MCPO Dardean's name, too. He had been a Master Chief Petty Officer under Senior Master Chief Birgitta Perry. Wounded four times at the Battle of Zulu Thunder, he, too, had been awarded the Corporate Medal of Valor. Ash had signed and submitted the recommendations for both the Briquet and Dardean. It was the highest military honor in the corporate forces.

"You can't tell it by looking at him," the Briquet said with a grin, "but this ol' SOB is younger than me."

"I used to have standards," Dardean winked at Ash.

"If you're a friend of the Senior Chief's, I bet you still do, Chief."

"Some," Dardean admitted, " — but they're my own. The service took most of the rest."

"He's known as Double-D. Why he didn't let them do some cosmetic on that ratty face of his, I'll never understand," Perry said. "He used to be handsome."

"I earned these scars," Dardean said. "I'm proud of 'em. They're who I am. Besides," he said with another wink, "it helps me get laid more than you might imagine."

"But you got your genes worked on," she continued to press.

"While I was laid up in recovery, figured I might as well — I wasn't getting any younger."

"It's an honor to meet you, Senior Chief," Ash said. "Any CVM holder is a man I admire."

"Sir," Chief Dardean said, "did the Senior Chief

happen to mention she was awarded a CVM, too?"

"No," Ash said with a small smile of admiration, "she seemed to have neglected that fact. But I remember signing her recommendation just as I did yours."

"And you got one, too, Sir," Perry said.

"I did. But mine was for standing on the command deck — didn't even get my hands dirty."

"Still, it was your planning and putting yourself and your ship in extreme danger that made what we did possible."

"The way I hear it, Sir," Dardean said, "you refused the CVM at first."

"I thought if they want to give this to me, every man-jack on board deserves one, as well."

"But the corporation wouldn't have that," the Briquet picked up the story. "I remember. They said your crew were just 'following orders.' But you wouldn't relent until they at least gave them all the Silver Galaxy. "

"It's all in the past now. Some stepped up — some didn't — and some died. That's the sum of war, I suppose," Ash said.

"Speaking for those of us who did, Sir," Master Chief Dardean added, "we're glad you were there and did what you did. That victory is more to do with you than with us. We were just dumb ass ground pounders. You were the brains behind everything."

"Kind of you to say, so, Master Chief."

"If you're ever doubtin' yourself, Sir," the former NCO went on, "get in the ring sometime and go a few rounds with the Briquet. If she doesn't kick your ass, you haven't lost your edge."

"I'll keep that in mind," Ash suppressed a smile. Perry looked as small as she was, but she could handle herself against anyone.

Senior Chief Perry seemed to want to change the subject. But before she could speak, Dardean said, "Right now, let's get in line before they run out."

"You must excuse him, Sir. Dardean's never met a meal he didn't like. That includes S rats." S rats were military slang for Subsistence Rations. Most who had been forced to survive even a day on the prepackaged meals considered starvation a possibly better alternative to what some were sure was actual ground rats.

"Comes from growing up hungry," Dardean said. "I don't recommend it."

"The Corporation saved Double-D from the streets," Perry said. "It was either the military or corporate work gangs."

"When shit is good," Dardean smiled, "it's damn good."

~

On their way to eat, Birgitta Genoveva Perry thought how strange life was. She had survived a privileged childhood and adolescence to become a street rat. Her successful parents, father an investment banker and her mother a haughty fashion designer, used her as a prop for family pictures. Otherwise, they shunting her upbringing to a series of disinterested nannies and live-in private schools. Although she had an above average IQ, she was bored with school by the end of her primary grades. As she lurched through puberty, she ran, sold, and used chemical compounds. Her customers and her herd were the other neglected progeny of professionally occupied parents. Sex she learned was, at best, a form of recreation.

Walking to their assigned chow hall with a man she considered almost a mythical figure, she remembered how being busted for drug use was the saving grace of her life. The criminal court judge who saw too many spoiled and irresponsible teens offered a choice of prison or corporate military. Her parents selected the latter option.

Through boot camp and advanced infantry training, Birgitta discovered the discipline and focus missing from her life. That she was a natural leader astounded her as much as the fact she and military life fit as if she were born to it.

She never saw her parents again, which satisfied them all. Birgitta was an embarrassment to her kin but on her own, she was steadily promoted and praised by the service she now considered her way of life. She learned how to fend off unwanted advances and accept those she desired. She developed a reputation as tough, agile, and quick of mind and reflexes. By the time of the Corporate War, she was a platoon NCO. She surprised herself with acts of bravery and a sincere intensity which propelled her through the ranks and earned her ribbons, metals, and respect.

DIXON DARDEAN HAD little trouble keeping up with Captain Kennett and the Briquet. He notice that they all walked in step. Darden felt he had emerged from the womb as a military brat. He followed in his divorced father's route after a turbulent secondary school career as a jock. Dixon's preferences ran to contact sports like rugby, wrestling, and karate.

In basic, he proved to be ahead of the average recruit. Athletic and already practiced in the orderly and correct manner to make a rack, clean and store uniforms and arms, it disappointed him to be assigned to cargo duty because of his strength. Within two years, however, he transferred to the tip-of-the-spear marines.

His first ass kicking came from his platoon sergeant — a woman known as the Briquet. He respected her for besting him and worked to prove himself worthy of her praise. The two served together in small engagements and were teamed again when the Corporate War erupted.

Dixon Dardean would follow any order Birgitta Perry ever gave him. Now he added Captain Kennett to that list. Through the war he found himself promoted always a little behind the Briquett. He became known as a reliable assistant team leader and was content with that position. He didn't mind the scars and wounds to his face and body, which he considered testimony to his willingness and ability to face any danger or obstacle.

CHAPTER NINE

After only a couple of minutes into their sparring, the other activity in the workout hatch had pretty much ceased. Current and ex-military were gathered around the rink where the intimidating form of Ash in a tee shirt and shorts doing a full-body contact bout with the camo sports bra and shorts dressed 'Briquet' Senior Master Chief Perry.

To the untrained eye, it looked to be a comfortable, forgone victory for the big man. Betting pools to that effect had sprung up, even offering three to one odds in Ash's favor.

But the former Captain understood that Perry was feeling him out as she wove and dodged his telegraphed strikes. He was not fooled as he was testing her. The betting stopped the first time the petite but brawny woman feigned a flying kick to his face only to turn it into a head scissor-lock twisting throw that put Ash flat on his stomach. She used her diminished size to her advantage in every move.

The session turned truly competitive after Ash bounced back and swept both of Perry's feet from under her. She hit the mat face first. The rebound speed of the pair astonished the onlookers. Several had switched their bets from one combatant to the other.

Ash used his size and balance to resemble an oak, but the former Master Chief could turn his strength against him with well-timed lunges carefully placed strikes with fists, knees, and heels.

One of Perry's body throws was turned back on her an instant after Ash slammed into the canvas, and he yanked Perry along with him, adding a knee to her chest before she could recover her balance.

The heels of her feet and that of her two palms gave the former Captain some solid jolts. But each was answered by an elbow slam or a throw, which found the previously ranked NCO slung into the ropes or banged into the mat. And yet, she always recouped with no apparent lasting effects.

She drew blood from Ash's nose, but he absorbed the blow and ended the bout in a move she'd never encountered. He spun her back to him with a shoulder kick and lifted her into the air by her bobbed hair. Off the mat with nothing on which to gain any purchase, Perry slammed down on the mat with Ash holding both of her wrists, his feet straddling her head. She double tapped Ash's fist as the signal of surrender. He released her.

The cheer which erupted wasn't applause for Ash or Perry but an appreciation for the skilled unarmed combat all had witnessed.

Ash's words of thanks couldn't be heard over the sound, but Perry understood. They both backed off and bowed to each other in respect.

IN THE OPEN shower the two combatants cranked the heat to just short of boiling. The steam billowed as they soaped and massaged their own aches. When they had turned their respective sprays to cold and caught each other's eye, they laughed. It had been a hell of a workout and tested them both — which, of course, had been the point.

They toweled off and sat on benches across from each other. Canvas burns, scrapes and scratches were abundant on both.

"You've certainly earned your reputation, Briquet," Ash said dabbing his nose to make sure the bleeding had stopped.

"And you've not lost your edge Sir," Perry smiled. "I'm either going to have to buzz cut my hair or find a strategy to combat that last move of yours."

"It'd be a shame to cut that hair," Ash said. "Did you consider using it to your advantage? You could have taken hold of my fist and swung yourself backwards and delivered a double kick upside my head?"

"I'd like to give that a try," she said thoughtfully. "But I'll need you to get me into that grip."

"Give me a couple of days," Ash said. "I'm glad to help, but you already pack a hell of a kick."

"I'll be a little tender for a few days myself. I won't even be up for sex. At least not my kind."

"You like it rough I take it?"

"Even with sex. If it's not rough, it's not sex," she grinned. "But I doubt you do rough."

"Not my style," Ash said.

"So what to do you call it?"

"Making love. Which," he said after a pause, "I must admit I haven't done in a long time."

"Oh, I remember long dry spells myself. But that's not my thing."

"I didn't think so."

"Either way," Perry said opening her locker and reaching for her clothes, "nothing helps heal or relax strained muscles like an exchange of bodily fluids."

"Agreed," Ash said getting to his feet and reaching for his own locker. "But it certainly seems we're not compatible."

"Shame," Perry pulled on her camo panties. "Well, Dixon is always available. And willing."

They shared a laugh.

"Are you two an item — or just friends with needs?"

"The latter. We've been through too much to be anything else. We have an understanding — and it works for us."

"As it should," Ash said. "It's no one else's business."

"However you do it — don't you miss it, Sir?"

A sadness came over Ash before he said, "You'd think so — but *no.* A key ingredient is missing for me."

"Let me guess. Trust." Perry could sense when she was in sensitive territory. "As you say, Sir, no one else's business."

***

Jaxlynn Shellanberger refused to be a victim. The heart shaped faced young woman with thick luminous copper color hair had served a year and a quarter in Bartholomew Lutz's harem. She had seen other young women who tried to defy Lutz by going limp and refusing to respond to the small brutal man. They were quickly sold off and disappeared.

She was not a virgin but faked being one during her first time with Lutz. He was still convinced. He relished inflicting pain and humiliation on women in particular. She had suffered through orgies and pairings of every description to please the vile pirate, but she kept her pride, her honor, and her self worth deep inside. The one thing she clung to was her now murdered grandfather's words, "Change is the only constant in this life. Never let events of the moment discourage you. Karma exists. Trust in time and change. Where you are now isn't were you have to end up."

In her meditation she resolved to never get pregnant by the monster who used her. She kept her peace and tried to help other girls — those who would be helped.

She became a trusted member of the harem under the evil watch of Arluna Ito. Ito was second in command to Lutz, taking the helm of a stolen battle cruiser originally manufactured by Hudson-Sturdivant — THE UNHOLY REVENGE. The woman looked to be in her early 40s, with shoulder length black hair, and spectacular bseasts which she displayed for all to enjoy and marvel. Her clothes all revealed as much caramel colored skin as possible. She often participated in multi-partner trysts with Lutz. The woman was feared more than she was respected. Everyone made way for Arluna when she walked or entered a room.

Jaxlynn was even given access to a computer tablet. Being an advanced computer major already in her second year of college, she wormed her way around the network of the pirate world. She was careful to disguise her trail and remain undetected in the rather antiquated system.

She read reports of the unexplained disappearance of THE STARDUST and the tepid reaction of the United Corporations military. She figured out where Deadwood was in the galaxy and never gave up. Such evil might grow, but she was convinced it would not endure. Still from where help might come she had no idea.

CHAPTER TEN

Over the next few weeks, Ash learned that Chief Dixon Dardean was a bit of a philosopher. The scar-faced former petty officer had done a considerable amount of reading during his 14 months of recovery from his wounds at Zulu Thunder. He and the Briquet shared almost every meal.

One evening during chow, he said. "I understand, Sir, that the unspoken — even unknown emotion is — we're scared — all of us survivors. None of us would admit it, and most of us don't even recognize it as such. They once called it 'battle fatigue' or 'flax happy' and later PTSD. Nobody wants to admit they have it. Once you get that tag, you're seen as a psychological cripple. But labeled or not, we'll never truly fit into normal society. I think that's the lot of certain generations over the centuries. Those who survived the Hundred Years' War were all damaged — even if they didn't directly participate in any fighting. Families and extended families — the hurt, the pain, even the guilt must have persisted for decades. Imagine those in the American Civil War — both sides. Even those they called 'The Greatest Generation' of World War II. Those who survived, won or lost any conflict — they all lived a very different life inside a very different world. It didn't and still doesn't matter to society — democracies and the socialist tyrannies — or corporations."

"It doesn't seem to have affected you two," Ash said.

"There's an old marine saying, Perry said, sitting back with a dark cup of coffee in her hands. "'You can soar with the eagles or you can shit with the pigeons.' We overcame — and if we have to, we will again and again."

"The question is," Dardean said, gathering up his cup, utensils, and tray, "is it better to survive or be vanquished? It's like Machiavelli's question for a ruler, 'Is it better to be feared or loved?'"

"And his answer for his prince," Ash said, "was

'to be feared.' Yet from our vantage point, we can see that such an approach has always delivered misery. We also can name the quantum leaps of civilizations have made when governed by justice and honesty."

"For the corporations, ultimately, it's always the bottom line," Perry stood taking her tray to the mess return window. "Wars are expensive but also profitable. As long as amounts almost balance — and the financial losses can be written off — nothing will change."

"It always amazes me," Ash said, "how the human cost is considered negligible. Look at us. Look at all the time and money they wasted in our training."

"Not to mention the expertise of the battle-tested and proven," Dixon said.

This paused the conversation as the three former combatants finished returning their dishes and left the mess hall.

In the passageway, Ash said, "And yet, look at us, we served — some would say we still serve — or at least do not obstruct our corporate masters. What does that make us? Are we a part of the system even now?"

Dixon Dardean frowned. "I suppose we are.

Although taking on the corporations is a fight many of us would take on until they killed us."

"But it's not economically worth it, like the Captain said," Perry said. "We are little more than digits on a spreadsheet. Our lives are of little value until they need us again."

"As long," Ash said, "as the philosophical 'bottom line' and 'whatever is best for the shareholders' dominated corporate thinking — I doubt anything will change. However, if the corporations call again, I, for one, won't answer. That's the point of my new venture."

"But who can escape it?" Dardean asked. "All the known universe is governed by the corporations."

"Sooner or later," Perry said, "some back room nerd is going to figure out how much they're losing by not having combat gear, vessels — all the infrastructure of war sitting around unused. And they'll find a reason to start up again. I'm willing to put my credits where my mouth is that none of them shut down their R&D departments. And look at us," the Briquet said. "We," she gestured to Ash, Dardean, and herself, "— eagles we may be — but for better or worse, war whores."

"Which is our problem," Dardean added. "We're whores without a war."

"Hooker without a house," Perry grinned. "Sluts without a street corner."

Ash said, "Are we? A friend recently told me I am a warrior. I consider you two the same. We could never be academics, middle management, or just laborers. Warriors are what we are. There are still some places where freedom is the goal of life — and warriors of good character are prized and even honored."

"I'd like to find such a place," Master Chief Dardean said.

The conversation stopped for a few moments until Ash seemed to change the subject.

"What would you two think about being fighting stevedores?"

"Stevedores — cargo loaders?" Perry asked.

"What's with the 'fighting' part?" Dardean wanted to know.

"I'm looking for certain people — former military — who can be stevedores as a day job but be ready to fight when needed — and we'd be looking for places to fight."

"Fight who?" Dardean and Perry asked at the same time. Perry added another comment, "We thought all the corporations had sworn off war — at least for a while."

"Pirates. Bartholomew Lutz to be specific. And we'd live by our own code."

"What code is that?" Perry asked.

Ash looked from Perry to Dardean and back to Perry before he spoke. "J.H.F. Justice, Honor, and Fidelity. I think each is self-explanatory."

"They are," Perry said, and Dardean agreed.

"I'd like to offer both of you jobs."

"I'm listening," she said, pausing.

"I've got a new ship — THE ERRANT — private. To the world it is a converted cargo hauler. But, trust me, it's much more. And I'm looking for an NCOIC," he said, looking at Perry meaning Non-Commissioned Officer In Charge. "And you'd need a good second — like Dixon."

"I'll speak for both of us," she said. "And it's affirmative, Sir."

Nothing more was said for several moments as Perry and Dardean considered everything Ash had said.

Finally, it was Perry who broke the silence by saying, "Bartholomew Lutz. That's a fight I want to be in."

"My God, do I hate those bastards." MCPO Dardean said, closing his eyes a moment while saying, "They kidnapped my younger brother —

turned him into a slave. And eventually killed him."

"We all know someone affected by those shitheels," Perry said grimly. There was a fire in Perry's eyes as she spoke.

"We'd also take on the corporations if they cross us."

"I'd sign up for that, too,"Dardean nodded. "I like the code."

"Where do we sign?" Senior Master Chief Perry said as Dardean agreed with a steady, stern nod of his head.

"Give me your hand. That's all I need from you."

The three of them solemnly shook hands in turn.

It was then that Ash asked, "Have either of you ever considered serving on an armed merchant vessel?"

"Armed?" Perry glanced at Double-D. "Isn't that an oxymoron?"

"Depends on who knows about it," Ash smiled. "It would be our little secret."

CHAPTER ELEVEN

A week later, Ash was eating his evening meal with his first hires when a young rated sailor with two stripes on his sleeve stepped up to the table, came to attention, and spoke.

"Captain Ash Kennett, CMV?" he asked.

Ash looked up. "Yes."

"Sir," he said, "your presence is requested immediately by Master Chief Quackenbush."

Ash got to his feet, wiping his mouth with a napkin. Without another word, he followed the sailor. They both quick marched out of the mess but broke into a dead run once they reached the passageway.

Two decks down, the sailor opened a hatch and shouted into it, "Attention! CMV on deck!"

By naval tradition, anyone holding the CMV deserved the military courtesy of the highest ranking officer in the room, on the site, or aboard a craft. Ash stepped through into the half-empty cargo storage compartment. A platoon of sailors stood at attention. Lashed to hooks on the wall with her back to those assembled was a young female sailor. Her blouse was ripped from her back. A Chief Petty officer stood only feet away from the prisoner with a double prong stun wand in her hand.

Across from the punishment stood the vessel's commanding officer wearing shoulderboards of a temporary captain.. His name tag read Younis. Next to him was the ship's senior most Master Chief, Quackenbush according to his name tag.

Ash understood immediately that this was a punishment detail. He stepped up to the Master Chief and spoke to him instead of the Lt. Captain.

"Master Chief, what's going on here?"

The Lt. Captain cocked his head in surprise as he arrogantly barked, "I am the commanding officer of this vessel."

"And you are at attention, Sir!" Ash snapped.

The officer came back to attention.

Ash asked again, "Master Chief?"

"Corporal punishment, Sir. Twenty-one strikes from a stun wand set to medium."

"What is the crime?"

"Operating an unauthorized still aboard a space going vessel, Sir."

"Twenty-one strikes?"

"Medium setting, Sir. Punishment dictated by the vessel's commanding officer."

"Twenty-one medium strikes will kill a person — or damn near it." Ash turned to the punishment sailor and said to her, "Turn off your device. Release the prisoner and have her cover-up."

Ash turned back to Quackenbush. "Master Chief, detail two sailors to accompany the prisoner to the brig. She is to be confined for two weeks."

"Aye, aye, Sir," the NCO said, pointing out two sailors in the group who helped the young woman secure her blouse. They each took an arm and helped her move. Obviously, she had already been shocked several times.

To the Master Chief Quackenbush, Ash next said, "Dismiss this detail but wait for me outside the hatch."

"Aye, aye, Sir," Quackenbush said.

Only when the space was left to Ash and Lt.

Captain Younis, did Ash step up to the ship's commanding officer. The officer still stood at attention but rage shown in his eyes.

"How dare you!" he shouted. "This is my ship and my command."

"Your very first command, I'd venture," Ash spoke calmly. "Garnered using family and political connections to jump ahead of any in your academy class, I have no doubt."

A little defensive the officer said, "It's still my ship and my command."

"Not a full Captain — only a temporary rank — Lieutenant Captain. But it's not your rank but your conduct that gives you away," Ash said.

"What does that imply?" Younis asked.

"Have there been reports of random, scattered security camera outages across the ship in the last week or so," Ash's question threw the young man.

After only a moment's hesitation, Younis replied, "Yes. What has that got to do with anything?"

"You are on the verge of being spaced, Lt. Captain. Sucked out of this ship through a faulty hatch where the cameras are inoperative. A seemingly empty stack of containers will fall on you just as the hatch opens and you will be purged into the icy vacuum of empty space. Alarms will sound, this ship and your two escort destroyers will stop, and they may find your body — but you'll already be dead by that point."

The young black officer swallowed hard, visualizing the events as Ash had described them. The images hit him so hard that his knees buckled and the Lt. Captain had to sit on the deck.

"When you leave here," Ash continued moments later when Younis looked up at Ash, "you will go straight to your cabin. You will remove yourself from the duty roster for the next three days. Your meals are to be delivered outside your door. You will also issue an order that you are not to be disturbed under any circumstance."

"W — why?" Younis asked in a weak voice.

"You, Sir, have some study and deep reflection to do. At the moment you are unfit for duty. Do you remember the Charlemagne Phishing Ambush from your history classes at the academy? That catastrophic battle cost the Imperium Corporation their entire fleet."

The Lt. Captain blinked and cut his eyes from one side to the other.

"What does that have to do with anything?"

"For the next three days, that fight will be your sole focus. With your connections, I'm sure you can obtain the original reports, including the four survivors' accounts. You are to read and reread those. Study everything about it. Also, from the ship's library, call up the book, Mutiny on the Bounty."

"I think I've seen some vids of that."

"No vids. Book. Read it."

"All right," the humbled young man finally said as he pushed himself to his feet. "What's this going to accomplish?"

"At the end of three days you'll emerge a better man and a better officer — or you'll be space debris before we reach Seafort." Ash let his words sink in and added, "Do you understand — completely?"

"Yes, Sir," came the barely audible response.

"Additionally," Ash said, "from now on, you will listen to and trust your NCOs. These are the people who have the first-hand experiences you will never possess. Give them the credit they earn and don't try to claim any of it for yourself. Let them know they can count on you to support them — even if and when mistakes are made. You are not their friend but their Captain — an often lonely, exposed, and misunderstood position. But since this is the life you have chosen, develop your own code of honor and conduct. Put the lives, the safety and the respect of your crew above all else — and live by it. Or you will die by the code you've been practicing so far. Understand that he who would be first must be willing to put himself last for his crew."

Lt. Captain Younis slowly nodded his head.

Ash said, "I'll see Master Chief Quackenbush outside. He'll escort you to your cabin. The rest is up to you. Learn some hard truths and profit from them — or die in arrogance and ignorance."

CHAPTER TWELVE

Former military were the last to disembark at Seafort from The WINDY CITY when it arrived at the space station. Not wanting to stand in any kind of line, Ash waited half a standard hour before making his way to the gangway hatch. He found Master Chief Quackenbush waiting for him. The NCO saluted Ash smartly and extended his hand for a shake after Ash returned the formal courtesy.

"I wanted to personally thank you, Sir, for responding to my request."

Ash nodded but said nothing.

"Just so you will know," the square-jawed Master Chief went on, "whatever you did or said in there to our C.O. has made a difference. He's got a long way to go — but, Sir, I think he now knows it."

"I understand your job, Master Chief — to make good officers out of material that's not always promising. To me, it's always been the hardest unwritten assignment in the service. I certainly owe more than I can ever repay to some very savvy NCOs."

The Master Chief gave Ash a quick nod of understanding.

"And the prisoner?" Ash asked.

"She's due out of the brig tomorrow. The Captain has brought up no other actions against her."

"Good," Ash said. "Good voyages and safe harbors, Chief."

"And to you, Captain? Will you be back in uniform soon?"

Ash stepped off and reluctantly saluted the new United Corporate emblem hanging limp outside the hatch. For the moment, he still lived under their banner.

"Yes, but a different one."

THE BRIQUET AND CHIEF DARDEAN awaited Ash as he finished with immigration.

"I didn't tell you," Ash said, "but you are both officially on the payroll — and you have an expense account for travel to Lima Nineteen. So get us a decent hotel."

"I'm liking this job, already," Dardean grinned through his bushy-mustache.

"Here's a station communicator," Senior Master Chief Birgitta Perry said, handing Ash a small coin. Ash pocketed it.

The communicator connected to his AI, and by touching the lobe of either ear, he would see a heads-up display in the corner of the left eye. This hologram was a history and directory of calls. The only contacts so far were Perry and Dardean.

"We'll need something more private and sophisticated." Ash said.

"I can get those," Perry said.

"A good place to hang our hats is The Peninsula," Chief Dardean said. "Not too pricey, but she has a fine restaurant and great reviews."

"Sounds good," Ash said. "Book us a suite."

"I'll call us a ride," Perry said, tapping her ear.

Seafort was a gigantic spinning wheel in space. It was 18 floors with vehicle traffic passages in both directions. It was possible to do the circumference at a jog in about a standard hour and a half on foot. Crossing corridors, one had to use the magnets in boots or shoes. The cross hall-ways met in the center of the wheel and offered access up and down the station. The control tower and admin offices were on the bottom of the center spiral where incoming and outgoing space traffic was directed. It was a well-kept sta-tion with lights changing by the minute to a 24-hour cycle of daylight and night.

The Peninsula Hotel was directly three decks above the cargo docks. The automated taxi ar-rived and took Ash, Perry, and Dardean on a swift but comfortable ride to the hotel's front doors. They checked in and were shown to a sub-dued suite with three bedrooms.

Down at the restaurant, the trio had a sub-stantial meal in a beautiful dining room.

"Our first job is to acquire a crew," Ash began as they ate.

"We're going to post a notice at the Merchant Marine site?" Dardean asked.

"We will, but I want it to go station wide. We're looking for primarily former military — regardless of corporate affiliation. The war's over. But a disciplined military will all be the same. Fighting ability and weapons knowledge are im-portant. The cargo part they can pick up — literally." The three shared a small laugh. "First of all," Ash continued, "I want reliable people you want to fly with and who you think will have your back. You must know some people on your own — people you'd be glad to serve with."

"People who can do more than move cargo, Captain?" the Briquet grinned.

"Yes, but that's not for publication. I don't want people who have loose lips — especially when they're drinking."

"We want to stay under the corporations' radar?" she asked.

"Everybody's radar. And when it comes to a fight, I want to know we have people who can do their jobs under fire."

"Got ya," Double-D said.

"Trust your gut more than anybody's record."

The two former NCO's liked those criteria.

"Send messages to former friends in arms. They can meet us here this week or later at Luna Ninteen. The station's called Xanadu Transit."

"You're going to hand-pick the officers and bridge crew, aren't you, Captain?" Perry asked.

"I will," he said. "But I want your input. If you know people who would be right for any of the jobs — ensigns to commanders — let me know."

"Gladly, Sir. But I do my best work below CIC

— not on the bridge. And you understand I've never handled cargo?"

"I was combat loadmaster before transferring to the ground pounders," Dardean said. "I'll teach you that part."

"Great," Ash smiled. "Dardean, you will be rated as Cargo Master Chief, and you will be Perry's second whenever needed. I've seen how you two work and interact together."

"Senior Chief," Ash said to Perry, "you have some cargo reading to do and some vids to watch. And follow Chief Dardean's lead. I expect you'll be up to speed by the time we reach Luna. Get to know the jargon. I plan to run THE ERRANT along military lines, so make sure you pick people who understand that."

"Aye, aye," the two said together.

"I'll send both of you a copy as soon as we finish here. Master Chief," Ash said to Dardean," print out one and go to the union hall and post it on the notice board. Any questions?"

"Dessert?" Dardean asked.

CHAPTER THIRTEEN

A sh was standing in the hotel suite's rear and had just finished talking to three young officers when Master Petty Officer Dixon Dardean approached with another man. Dardean towered over the shorter and younger man beside him, but both had a commanding military presence. It was late one afternoon as they were finishing their recruiting efforts for the week.

"Begging your pardon, Captain," Dardean said as he and the man beside him popped a smart salute, "I want to introduce you to Petty Officer Wyatt Light. He's the best dog robber I've ever known."

A 'dog robber' in military parlance had come

to mean someone proficient at acquiring whatever his or her unit needed by whatever means. The term 'midnight requisition' often accompanied any description of such a person and their activities. Every team needed a dog robber, but few ever acknowledged that there was in their ranks anyone who would fit that description.

Ash returned the salute before offering his hand. Petty Officer Wyatt Light was deeply tanned, with ears almost 90 degrees to his head. He wore what looked like a perpetual smile.

"Petty Officer," Ash said, "welcome."

"It's an honor to meet you, Sir."

"Wyatt here," Dixon said, "can acquire anything, and I do mean anything available on concise notice."

"That is a formidable ability," Ash said. "And I'll ask you no questions."

"And I'll tell you no lies," Wyatt Light finished the old saying.

"I believe we understand each other. With Master Chief Dardean's recommendation, I will assume we are on the same screen."

"Focused and locked, Sir."

"He's already arranged passage for all of us to Luna Nineteen," Dardean said as if to prove his point, "at half the rate Senior Chief Perry and I were able to find."

"Well done," Ash nodded. "When do we depart?"

"End of the week. Saturday at 1300. THE BETTY RUTH. She's a passenger carrier. Dock 14 — Sword Dock."

"Excellent," Ash said. "Looking forward to working with you, Petty Officer Light."

"And I with you, Sir." Light saluted and exited the room.

Dardean stayed behind to say to Ash, "I mean it, Sir. Anything, anytime. He works magic."

"What are the accommodations he has for us?"

"Single rooms for all the officers and senior NCOs we have by then, doubles for the other Petty Officers, and four apiece for the rest. Plus, there is an empty freight bay we have for training and anything else we need."

"He lives up to his billing."

"As for the rest of the crew," Dardean said, screwing up his face, "— some are really out of shape. But it's nothing the Briquet and I can't correct on our trip."

"I like the way you think, Master Chief. THE BETTY RUTH — berth 14 — 1300 hours. Sword Dock."

"Aye, aye, Sir. Any other needs at this time?"

"Replicators. Industrial size — large and medium. We're going to need weapons and tactical gear. And, Master Chief Dardean," Ash said, turning to the more senior NCO. "Could you locate someone with design skills? We have no uniform beyond black coveralls."

"Aye, aye," the brawny non-com said.

"Understood, Sir," Light added. "I'll get right on it."

By the end of the week, they had assembled a crew of 117 so far. Six officers were in the mix, and the rest were rated noncommissioned petty officers, equal to three-stripe army sergeants, PFCs and Lance Corporals. As Ash had explained it, these people needed to be able to be cross-trained Sigma Fi certified. Sigma Fi was what had become the standard military nomenclature for special forces operators. They would each have to be able to work on their own or in 7 member teams.

Each team was made up of an Ops Detachment (OD) with a CO (Commanding Officer), a rated lieutenant who was equal to an army captain. Each person had to be a master in the arts of unconventional warfare and standard military tactics. Officers had to be able to function in the role of any other Sigma Fi team member. The detachment CO also had to be able to advise an indigenous battalion-size combat force. So far, only two of those who applied met these criteria.

The Assistant DO's Assistant Captain would be rated a Brevet Ensign (temporary) who was to be chosen from within each team's enlisted ranks.

The OD's Team Petty Officer's rank was a Master Petty Officer like CPO Dardean. This team member was to be the most experienced Sigma Fi in each detachment to be placed as the senior NCO of the OD.

The Assistant Operations and Intelligence Petty Officer was rated a Petty Officer first class. This slot's duties were to be knowledgeable in advanced SF techniques, including intelligence collection and processing and target analysis.

A Weapons Petty Officer had to be an expert in the employment and use of all known weapons systems, from small arms to massive robotic military machines. The weapons Petty Officer also had to assist the OD's operations Petty Officer in preparing training and operational plans.

The Engineering Petty Officer had to be

highly skilled in the planning and constructing of buildings, fortifications, and bridges along with their demolition. This team member had to know destructions from hand installed mines to creating and using improvised munitions. Additionally, these Petty Officers controlled the unit's robots and drones.

The Medical Petty Officer had to be proficient in not only human but also animal physiology. This Petty Officer was a specialist in trauma management, infectious diseases, cardiac life support, and surgical procedures. He could also perform essential veterinarian medicine. Medical Petty Officers provided emergency, routine, and long-term medical care for their teams and associated allied members and host nation personnel. They trained, advised, and directed the detachment's routine, emergency, and preventive medical care. They can also establish field medical facilities to support detachment operations.

The Comms Petty Officer was the OD's link to the rest of the world. This person had to be an expert in sending and receiving critical communications to the OD's command and control elements. Communications Petty Officers were familiar with cryptographic systems, burst outstation, and laser point to point networks. Additionally, they knew antenna theory and radio wave propagation and the installation, operation, and maintenance of all comm gear.

It was clear some would need additional training as well as cargo handling skills. But after a week at Seafort, it wasn't a bad start. The next step was to move to Luna Ninteen and THE ERRANT.

CHAPTER FOURTEEN

The craft with which CPO Light had made arrangements was THE BETTY RUTH. It was a commercial cargo and passenger ship registered as independent as opposed to being a corporation flagged ship. It had had a couple of minor encounters with would-be pirates but had escaped due to its engines' power and the Captain's wits.

The Captain looked to be in his late 40s, but the rumor was he had been nearly 70 when he had taken his first genetic treatments. He had a full head of hair, and a smartly trimmed mustache of light brown that went well with his dark complexion.

"I was a tug captain for 50 years," he told Ash

when he welcomed the Sigma Fi warriors aboard. "Been at this for about half that long, but I like this much better." Swain smiled.

"There are some pirates about — or some who want to be. They have stolen ships with poor leadership — but one day, they'll pull something off. I'm damn glad to have you and your people with us, Captain Kennett — you know — just in case."

"I do understand, Captain," Ash replied. "And if there is an incident, we will be ready to repel boarders."

"Excellent. I couldn't ask for more. Hope you like your accommodations."

"They will be fine, Captain. Can you please see that your civilian passengers don't come near the cargo bay we're using for training?"

"You have my word, Captain. And I'd like to see you come up to the bridge as your time permits."

"It will be my pleasure," Ash said as the two men shook hands.

OVER THE FIRST week and a half of the trip, Senior Chief Perry made a believer out of all of those who had forgotten the rigors of special military operations. Physical training, boxing, mixed martial arts, and the ancient form of Krav Maga were combined into a self-defense program and offense program.

Mostly the men and women who had made up the unit were former military who found they did poorly as civilians following the corporate wars. Military life's discipline and structure suited them and allowed them to thrive — even if several had to struggle to regain their former weight and agility.

Half of the cargo training bay was covered with pads for combat training, but two boxing rings were also constructed. A firing range for small arms had to be reinforced before it could be used. By the end of the first week, a roundabout running track as well as weight lifting benches were in place. Ball courts for different games became centers for recreation.

All this time, Ash, his new officers, and Senior Master Chief Perry were evaluating and beginning the process of building Sigma Fi teams.

Ash was often invited to the bridge by Captain Swain. They talked about the cargo-hauling business. Since Swain had been military early in his career, the two men understood each other.

One morning, ship time, a predatory ship suddenly uncloaked parallel and running starboard of THE BETTY RUTH.

"This is THE PESTILENCE!" came an unbid communication as a black pirate flag flashed onto the comms video screen. "Come to a full stop and make the following air locks ready for umbilicals! You will be boarded! You are under our guns! Deviate, and you will be blown to dust!"

CHAPTER FIFTEEN

L t. Studebaker, black-haired, average height and fit but not overly muscled, took one-fifth of the boarding party. Lt. J.G. Lina Jewitt, slender and well proportioned for her frame, commanded the second group; Master Chief Dardean the third. The Briquet took the remaining 26.

"Arm yourselves with combat knives and laser pistols set to stun," Studebaker ordered the main body. "The ranking NCO of each group will carry a close-quarters rifle."

The crew broke up and armed themselves according to the lieutenant's specifications and quickly reassembled.

"Gamma Team," Studebaker nodded toward Master Chief Dardean's group, "take deck six airlock. Do not let these bastards get to the passengers!"

"Beta Team," he indicated Lt. Jewitt's group, "deck 10. They CANNOT get to the engine room!"

"Alpha," he addressed his group of about 40, "we are headed to deck 4. They're after the bridge — and they won't make it!"

"Master Chief Perry take up a position behind Lt. Jewitt's unit. You will be the advance boarding team."

Studebaker scanned the black workout uniformed crew. "Follow your team leaders! Now!!"

The units sprinted off behind their leaders.

Perry told her group to suit up in armor and draw weapons. They would assemble out of sight. They would not move out until Captain Kennett gave them the word.

CAPTAIN SWAIN'S face lost all of its color. Only slightly above a whisper he turned to his helmsman and ordered, "Full stop."

"Full stop, Captain," the young man at the navigation station acknowledged.

Swain's next order was calm and totally in control of himself. "Give me full shipboard communications."

The communications officer, a round woman who looked to be in her mid-thirties with a single braided purple and yellow strand of hair on the left side of her head, pressed a button.

"Full shipboard communications," she said.

It took a second for Captain Swain to gather his thoughts and then he spoke. "This is the Captain speaking! All guests please return to your quarters immediately and secure your cabin door and yourself in your emergency seating! Strap yourself in!" Swain took a breath and continued, "All crew, general quarters! Repeat — passengers to their cabins and secure yourselves in emergency seating — all crew to general quarters! We are being halted by an unauthorized but threatening vessel to our starboard! I will keep you informed as the situation develops!"

Captain Swain sank down into his chair as his shoulders sagged. His eyes glanced up and saw Ash. The former military Captain had been called to the bridge as the first sighting of the suspicious approaching vessel. Ash grasped the situation and held up an index finger as if saying, "Just wait."

"We are being hailed, Captain," the young comms officer said to Swain.

"Open a channel," Swain ordered and then spoke to the pirate chief on the large main screen. "Who is this?"

"I am Captain Percival Randsom. Obey my commands and you will live to see another day. Disobey me one whit and I will destroy you!"

The face looked more like a woman than a man but the voice was in the lower registers. Randsom's head was shaved and both ears were festooned with jewels and ear rings.

The nasty and demanding voice came through connection once more. "We will attach umbilicals at your forward air lock on decks four, a midships on deck six, and starboard rear deck 10! Set your magnetics to accept connections!"

Ash stepped back against the front wall of the bridge behind the command crew's comm screens — out of the range of the camera that was focused on Captain Swain. Taking charge, Ash looked at the comms officer and pointed to his ear and then swiped a flat hand across his throat. The woman understood and cut the outgoing audio feed.

Next Ash tapped his ear. "Lt. Studebaker, Senior Master Chief Perry," he said in a low but commanding voice. Studebaker was the ranking lieutenant they had hired at Seafort.

Lt. Studebaker and SMPO Perry responded.

"Lt., prepare to repel borders. Let them inside and then close the air locks and attack. Senior Chief Perry, prepare an armored team to take control of the other ship. You will need two teams — one fore and one aft." Ash repeated the air lock locations where the pirates would board. "Completion signal is 'Saturn.' Repeat, 'Saturn.'"

"Aye, aye," came the replies from Lt. Studebaker. Ash knew it was now in their hands.

Finally Ash spoke to Capt. Swain quietly.

"My teams are moving to intercept."

Looking at the Comms officer Ash said, "If the pirate captain begins speaking, open the link instantly." The woman nodded. "Can you jam their audio and video feeds once they're aboard?"

"Aye, aye," she said. "Should I wait until they close the outer air locks?"

"Exactly," Ash nodded. "But you can see what channel I'm using. Leave it open."

Turning to the young man at the helm Ash asked, "How good are you at your job?"

Without moving his lips Swain said, "Cyrel can make this ship dance on the head of the pin."

"Good," Ash said. Then speaking to the helmsman he said, "On my order I want you to begin spraying landing foam and using our thrusters to spin us around THE PESTILENCE with our underside facing that ship and continuing to spray."

Landing foam was a standard component of all vessels. It was an extruded mix of chemicals designed to create a bed up to two miles long to soften the impact of a hard landing on any surface. The froth would be adjusted depending on atmosphere (or lack of one), gravity or terrain.

"Set the foam hardness to 'Tango slash Instant,'" he ordered and the helmsman acknowledged.

Ash turned to the comms officer, pointed to his ear again and shot his thumb out of his fist.

Captain Swain took that as his cue to speak.

"Air locks enabled for attachment." Swain reported to the pirate captain.

Ash could make out the reflected image from one of the sensor screen cameras showing three umbilicals thrust out from THE PESTILENCE and connected to the sides of THE BETTY RUTH. Within moments the air lock on the other

ship opened and pirates in environmental protection suits and armor moved out and floated thru
the tubes. There were about a dozen or less in
each group.

There was nothing more Ash could do now
but wait.

CHAPTER SIXTEEN

The translucent umbilicals shot out from THE PESTILENCE and impacted the sides of THE BETTY RUTH at the prepared airlocks. It took 34 seconds for each tube to be pressurized from its mother ship until the airlocks at the base of each on the pirate's side opened. A dozen ill-dressed pirates emerged into each gangway and pulled themselves along the links.

The pirates wore an assortment of old military combat armor, some from two wars back. All were encased in some sort of space protection and fighting gear. Each had been repainted to appear vicious and more dangerous than they really were. They carried laser pistols of different manufacture, a variety of rifles — any of which, if fired, would pierce the umbilicals or even the hulls of either vessel.

When each group reached the outer airlock doors of their assigned target, they waited. A leader from each activated the opening lever, and THE BETTY RUTH's thick outer thresholds slowly opened.

The pirates crowded aboard into the airlocks and closed the outer hatches. They had to wait for the pressurization to equalize before they opened the inner hatches and stepped aboard.

On deck 6, as on the others, the pirates were confused when their comm gear began malfunctioning as the airlocks pressurized. They were banging on their helmets and checking their bodcams even as the inner doors parted.

One pirate took his position just inside the passageway with his back to the airlock doors as the confused party stepped aboard. Giving up on their comms, the rest of the dozen invaders hurried towards a closed elevator at the end of the passageway. The call button was pressed, and they waited.

A moment later, only one deck up, the elevator doors opened and the pirates discovered themselves facing Chief Dardean and his group of black coveralled Sigma Fi's. The SF team was prone, on their knees and standing, tightly massed and all with weapons pointed outward. They fired in unison, and the pirates dropped like a flock of electrocuted birds.

Elsewhere, one SF with a rifle, kneeling at the SF group's left edge, fired a single shot killing the pirate guard who emerged from the airlock door. The rest of the raiders were cut down by the awaiting SF team.

Chief Dardean opened his comm to his CO. He said, "Gamma —Saturn."

ON DECK 10, the airlock was large to accommodate machinery and large loads. It opened into a loaded cargo bay. Lt. J.G.Lina Jewitt had positioned her force behind boxes and crates.

The cocksure pirates were confounded when their comms suddenly went dead. When the inner airlock doors opened, they stepped out -- their attitude had changed. Now wary and looking in all directions, their confidence had been shattered. Their leader, who had the newest of their gear, wore an exoskeleton on top of his snake-skin painted armor. They exited the airlock in a cluster but spread out when their leader began shoving them in different directions.

They proceeded carefully, aiming their weapons up and down the stacked crates and boxes. It wasn't until they neared the lift that they came together again.

On Lt. Jewitt's signal, her team rose and fired in unison, and the pirates collapsed. The marksman of her group also took out their remaining guard at the airlock door. Her squad then leaped down and disarmed the invaders.

Jewitt responded only a moment after Chief Dardean. "Beta — Saturn."

JUST AS ON the other decks, the pirate band coming to take over the bridge and command of THE BETTY RUTH were confounded when their communications suddenly failed. The elevator to the bridge opened only a few yards away from the airlock, and the wide hallway was open and clear.

Using hand signals, this group's leader motioned on his pirates to take up a position by the airlock. The rest of the invaders moved, stepping slowly as they approached the lift.

The passage was empty, and no threat appeared.

As Lt. Studebaker flashed a penlight, his squad dropped from ceiling tiles firing their stun pistols. The ranking NCO sighted through his heat-seeking sight and took out the airlock guard without having to move. She pumped three armor-piercing rounds into the pirate and watched the figure drop. Then the sniper dropped through the hole in the ceiling tile and kicked the dead guard's weapon away.

Not another shot was fired on any deck.

On the bridge, Ash heard, "Alpha — Saturn."

ASH RECEIVED his final confirmation before nodding to the helmsman. Instantly THE BETTY RUTH disengaged the three umbilicals and whipped under THE PESTILENCE jettisoning a flood of yellow-green slime from the merchant's nozzles in her belly. The artificial gravity kept all aboard THE BETTY RUTH unaware of the sudden movement.

The profound confusion of the pirate captain could only be imagined. First, he had lost all audio, video, and location connections with his boarding crew, then his umbilicals were disconnected, and the unarmed merchant ship was whirling under and around him. Compounding his confusion was the blacking out of all his external sensors as landing form streamed from the other ship as it twirled around him.

"Quickly to port," Ash commanded as soon as they were back to THE BETTY RUTH's beginning position.

The now coated and blinded THE PESTILENCE fired one of its cannons, which only resulted in a sizable hole in its side and a gushing of pressurized atmosphere and pirates' bodies being flung into the cold stillness of space.

"Reposition to our original position," Ash ordered. Into his comm, he spoke, "Senior Master Chief, you are a go!"

From the now sealed airlocks on decks 4 and 10, SMC Perry opened the outer doors of tier 4 while her appointed leader for the second team did the same on deck 10.

The armored and armed marines jetted out of the airlocks toward the first and third umbilicals' open ends. To an outside observer, THE PESTILENCE was in a cacoon.

THE BETTY RUTH moved and from its nose spurted landing foam into THE PESTILENCE's engine nozzle. THE BETTY RUTH executed and flat twirled around THE PESTILENCE with its belly always facing the enemy craft. It ended up just above the enemy vessel and continuing to cover it with foam.

"To the rear of that ship!" Ash ordered.

THE BETTY RUTH shot back until it was behind its rival.

"Eject forward foam!" Ash commanded.

In moments, THE PESTILENCE looked like a cocooned insect with three slowly and awkwardly twisting limbs. The foam hardened, and both blinded all the enemy's sensors and also blocked its engines and weapons. The desperate attempt to fire one energy weapon from amidship caused an explosion, which created a gaping hole on the port side of THE PESTILENCE. It was gushing atmosphere and unable to move. Automatic doors on board must have sealed because the belch of air only lasted a few seconds.

Ash stepped around the bridge crew's screens, glancing up at the main comm screen, which now displayed the forward view from the vessel's nose. Ash addressed Captain Swain. "They are blind, deaf, and stranded."

"Well done, Captain," the old salt gushed. "And excellent work, my friends," he said to his crew.

CHAPTER SEVENTEEN

The Briquet, Senior Master Chief Birgitta Petty, led the first team of a dozen in their fights. The component was fully armored with gear printed from the onboard printers. Likewise, each was dressed in full body armor, armed with a slug, laser and pulse rifle, stun pistol, and combat knife. The team followed SMC Perry as they jetted from THE BETTY RUTH's forward airlock to the drifting end of the forward umbilical.

Once Petty latched onto one of the umbilical's handhold, she pulled herself up the tube. She withdrew a device from a leg pack and focused a beam on THE PESTILENCE's forward airlock.

The signal from the handheld gadget degaussed and deactivated every sensor on the outside of the airlock. She then hauled herself to the airlock door and awaited the rest of her team.

~

THE SECOND SF boarding team was lead by Petty Officer Miguel Cyril. The swimmer-fit, agile, and dark, mustached Operational Detachment leader took his team up the third umbilical. Like Senior Master Chief Perry, CPO Cyril used a handheld device to block the camera and sensors outside THE PESTILENCE's aft airlock.

When CPO Cyril's team was gathered, he twisted the handle opening the outer door. With all weapons at the ready, the team surged into the airlock. Once in, CPO Cyril pressed the button and pressurized the airlock, and opened the interior door.

A few disorganized pirates awaited with handheld weapons, which they fired as the inner airlock door parted. Protected by their armor, the Sigma Fi team boldly returned fire and leaped into the littered passage.

The few pirates who had taken cover behind barrels and crates were engaged in hand to hand by the SF team, in short-lived fights — all of which ended in dead pirates.

CPO Cyril's team stormed down the hall and took stairs to the engine room. Rather than fight, the pirates threw up their hands or hit the deck with open hands and widespread arms and legs.

Into his helmet mic, CPO Cyril announced, "SF team Epsilon — Saturn. Repeat Saturn."

SMC PERRY SPLIT her team in half. Six went with her, and the other half took the second hallway to the starboard bridge door. On her signal, one of her team members stepped forward and attached a conical shaped charge to the door's center. Punching a button on it one side ignited a series of green LEDs, which flickered on in a circle around the explosive. The team members nodded toward Perry and stepped back to their places in the assault group.

"Fire in the hole," the Briquet communicated to her part of the team. They all turned away from the door. A moment later, the conical shaped charge's LEDs changed from green to red. Then the explosive went off.

The Briquet dove and tumbled through the

smoke. She came up on one knee, weapon ready. She shot and killed the figure near the captain's chair. What she didn't know was that it was not Percival Randsom.

The shaved head and jeweled eared pirate captain had snatched his comms officer out of her chair when THE PESTILENCE began losing signals from his boarding teams. The substitute, a heavily tattooed and file-pointed tooth, heavyset woman, had staggered back to the captain's chair. There she died.

Randsom had ducked when the port side bridge hatch splintered but came up pulling his laser pistol when the starboard hatch exploded. The second half of the boarding team's team leader executed a move, just like SMC Perry's. But it was a sharpshooter still in the passage who identified Randsom at the comm console. The shooter shot him in his shaved head. The small round stayed intact until it was inside the pirate captain's skull. There the slug detonated and scrambled everything between the jaw and the crown of the skull into mush. Randsom dropped like a soaked towel.

The three other bridge crew members threw themselves to the deck, face down, legs, arms, and fingers all spread to prove themselves defenseless.

When SMC Perry stood and surveyed the scene, she keyed her mic and announced, "Delta — Saturn. Moving to secure the vessel."

~

THE BRIQUET'S team left two team members to guard the bridge and the prone pirates there. The rest moved down the passageways headed aft. They began to sweep down through the decks and back towards engineering. Likewise, CPO Cyril and his SF half of the boarding team cleared the aft decks and every compartment before moving forward to link up with team Perry's unit.

THE PESTILENCE was the picture of a sloppy and neglected ship. The place was a mess in every regard. It was evident the crew had little if any discipline and not a sense of order and hygiene. Once the craft had been secured, the first order of business would be to set the cleaning robots to work and muster all hands to the task of spit and polish.

The seized bridge crew were pushed first down every unexplored passageway and compartment. It quickly became evident that they had nothing to fear of booby traps. Every hand on

THE PESTILENCE and not on the bridge or in engineering had wanted to be a part of the raiding, raping, and pillaging party.

When the boardings teams hooked up and the "all secure" signal transmitted back to THE BETTY RUTH, the captives were herded into an empty cargo hold to await their comrades.

BACK ON THE BETTY RUTH, the three groups of pirates for decks 4, 6, and 10 were bound, their wounds treated, and their dead compatriots spaced. The living and the walking wounded were then corralled and marched back across their umbilical from deck 10 to THE PESTILENCE. There they were united with the rest of their crew in the guarded cargo hold. For the first day, they were provided with neither water, toilets, or bedding.

Captain Swain told Captain Kennett the captured ship belonged to him. "It was your people who conquered it."

"Space maritime law says it belongs to the Captain of the vessel who took it. We work for you, Captain. Legally we are, at this moment," Ash pointed out, "members of your crew."

"You were passengers," the old salt countered. "It is your prize, and I'll have it no other way. Besides, how can the damn thing even be moved? It's encased in landing foam. It's not going anywhere without a lot of EVA work."

"Tell you what," Ash said after thinking it over a moment, "Loan me some EVA suits, and we'll get her ready to move — and even get her ready for your fleet."

"My fleet," the shaved head and full-bearded Captain said.

"Wouldn't you like a second ship — a sister ship to THE BETTY RUTH? It would enlarge your business."

"I can't argue with that, Captain, but claiming it doesn't seem right to me."

"Then what do you say to a partnership."

"Partnership?"

"This was a training exercise for my people. I propose a sixty — forty split — you the sixty. We the silent 40."

"That's one hell of a deal," Swain grinned. "But how do we even move it first?"

"I have a backup pilot and some engineers to crew her. We'll need to use your tractor beam and string a cable to get her underway."

"Done!" Swain agreed, and the two men shook

hands. "But be advised, my tractor beam is made for cargo and passenger luggage — not hauling another ship.

"We'll make it work," Ash said.

CHAPTER EIGHTEEN

Ash informed his assembled crew in a different empty cargo hold of THE PESTILENCE, "You are now all part owner of this vessel. After she's refitted she will sail again — and we all share in 40% of her profits — as long as she sails."

A loud cheer went up as the surprised warriors looked from one to the other, not clearly understanding.

"By law, this ship now belongs to Captain Swain. But he has generously offered a partnership, which makes each of us an equal partner of forty percent. I will set up accounts for you all. Your payments will be deposited into your accounts according to your rank. As for those who died in our first action — their share will go to their families. That will be our policy going forward."

Another cheer filled the compartment.

"Captain Swain will throw us a tow line, and we'll soon be underway. We will provide our own pilot and engineering crew. CPO Dardean's task is to keep the pirates as miserable as they would have any captives they might have obtained. I would like them ready to cooperate with the corporate police when we turn them over. Our job is to make this bucket of crap something worth a new name."

Ash turned to his two officers. "Lt. Studebaker, you and the NCOs will see to scouring and polishing of the interior of this ship. Lt. Jewitt, you will stay in your EVA suits and construct a boom from THE BETTY RUTH and attach a cable to us."

"Aye, aye, Sir," both responded.

"I expect to be underway within three hours."

WITH THE PESTILENCE now shrouded in a hardening landing foam, Lt. J.G. Lina Jewitt took half of her crew to the EVA assignment. Both teams now were still in EVA suits. Jewitt's people hacked away at the coating to make a tow cable connection possible. There was no way to accomplish the task of freeing the engine nozzles without spending weeks at the job.

Once the cable's opening was clear, she assigned three lines to an external bracket port side of THE BETTY RUTH clear of her thrusters. The second half of her team, led by MCO Perry, constructed the boom out of a rear cargo hold. Captain Swain used his towing beam to the other ship, which helped, but this under-powered ray could not support THE PESTILENCE.

MCP Dardean was put in charge of the prisoners. Dixon Dardean made sure the only face the captured pirates saw was his terrifying and frightening face. He did provide them with water rations but no toilets for the first day. The former pirates had to use an open container to serve as a unisex privy in the center of their confinement. The rank smell was theirs to endure.

When the boom and cable were in place and tested, THE BETTY RUTH began to move and bring the almost dead ship with her. The pilot, Ensign Javon Haygood, had to use the few maneuvering jets of the pirate craft. The first EVA team had located and cleared them to ensure the prize vessel stayed beside and to the mother ship's port side.

~

THE REST of the voyage to Tatius was relatively uneventful.

Onboard THE BETTY RUTH one lucky reporter got an exclusive, which he recorded and broadcast within 7 hours. Two novelists began work on new books, one adventure and one a romance, while several would-be screenwriters began to crank out hopeful stories for vids.

Ash's command had to repair some of the cleaning robots and use considerable elbow grease before THE PESTILENCE was again an inhabited craft. Being part owners of the ship made the effort not so much a chore as it might have been.

The engineering crew went to work on the pirate's still clogged engines.

~

TATIUS WAS a multi corporation terraforming project. It took 20 years to accomplish the job on an exoplanet its size, about three-quarters the size of Earth. Beyond the natural warmth of the system's star, Tatius was supplied with sunlight from the solar gathering Collector station in a stationary orbit over the rotating planet. The Collector was composed of a processing and projecting hub and mammoth array of solar panels. This celestial satellite had been operating for the past five years. The terraforming chore below was nearing completion. The most interesting fact about Tatius was not that it was outside the so called "Cinderella" zone but that it was only one of the system's twenty-three moons. Some of the in-system moons were only a few miles in diameter.

***

Moon number 19 was about Jupiter's moon Callisto's size, twice the Earth's moon but not as large as Ganymede.

Above Luna Nineteen, orbiting in a stationary position, was Xanadu Transit. It was a significant spaceport and shipyard. The Hudson-Sturdivant Corporation owned the site. Before and during the Corporate War, the H-S Corp centered its business model on weapons and ship production. After the conflict ended, its directors decided to redirect corporate efforts. When it signed onto the Luna nineteen project, it claimed the solar collection and space station as its responsibility and contributions. A significant part of Xanadu was the shipyard, but the entire station was laid out as a commercial venture to attract and facilitate trade.

Xanadu Transit had been the turnaround destination of THE BETTY RUTH for the last four standard years. Her regular route took her across the Kermerus galaxy bringing this outpost new and spare parts, food, and workers. In exchange, it hauled back an assortment of ores from nearby asteroid miners.

The planet Tatius wasn't yet to be inhabited by humans, but there were certain algae, a few low-level insects, and a few aquatic and amphibian species that were thriving. The atmosphere still needed another year's growth before it was considered ideal for advanced insects and mamuals.

Before THE BETTY RUTH reached either the Tatius solar system's outer gravity, much less Luna Nineteens's pull, it disconnected from THE PESTILENCE. The still blind pirate ship was flung toward the planet by itself. Once it reached Tatius's top atmosphere, it began a steady insertion nose-first. The rock-tough landing foam coating had solidified. The ship started to heat, glowing red and peeling off in sizable chunks of its encrusted covering. As the craft gathered speed and friction as it pummeled through the maturing atmospheric barrier, it was being scrubbed spotless.

Prominent clumps of foam broke off from the ship's outer skin and were thrown away in fiery clods. Other pieces began to chip off and burn away until at least the front of THE PESTI-LENCE forward sensors cleared and came back online.

On the bridge, with all the crew strapped in tightly. The pilot, Ensign Javon Haygood, had been a fighter jockey but assured Ash he could handle THE PESTILENCE. He glanced back at Ash in the Captain's chair. Ash nodded to the dark-skinned young man, who made some quick adjustments to his controls.

Gracefully THE PESTILENCE flipped 180 degrees and continued streaking through the atmosphere aft first. After several more jolts, the vehicle's propulsion nozzles were chipped and burned away. For fully two minutes, THE PESTI-LENCE continued at this trajectory. When no more foam pieces were hurled past the frost view screens, the pilot didn't even look back at Ash as he readjusted the ship's attitude back to nose-first. When Lt. Haygood did look at Ash once more, he said, "I believe we are clean, Captain."

Through the ship's command intercom, Ash ordered, "Engineering. Start engines."

Only seconds passed before the deep rumble of the ship's powerful main plant came online. Lt. Haygood had full navigational control, and the vehicle maneuvered away from the planet and back up through the atmosphere. The g-forces were tremendous at first but soon relaxed to a tolerable level.

Two hours later, THE PESTILENCE came within visual range of Xanadu Transit, above Luna Nineteen.

"Captain Swain," Ash said over their communications, "we're on our way."

"Thank you, Captain Kennett," Swain said. "There'll be tugs and a berth awaiting you."

CHAPTER NINETEEN

THE BETTY RUTH had already docked in a closed berth and had requested a place for THE PESTILENCE. Captain Swain had alerted authorities of the craft's arrival and to the captured pirate cargo aboard his ship. Swain met the security lieutenant in charge of the detail. He introduced the young officer to impressive CPO Dardean. The filthy and dejected lot of former space raiders was unceremoniously force-marched into awaiting detention vehicles.

THE PESTILENCE was also met before it achieved station nearby. Two Scorpion fighters escorted her to a military pier on the bottom-most tier of the station. There, surrounded by a military police company, the ship was locked into a docking space and a sealing door secured behind it.

Ash opened the ship to the thorough inspection of the local authorities. Before he left the former pirate craft, Ash released his crew on a twenty-four hour liberty to what facilities had been completed on the station. Ash joined Captain Swain at the Station Master's office to sort out ownership of the captured ship.

Captain Swain's problem was to move THE PESTILENCE to the shipyards for repairs, refitting, and renaming.

Captain Swain was with the rotund Station Master, a woman with as many extra pounds as she had accumulated date chips on her large desk. She was a good-natured woman Swain knew well, and they were embracing as Ash stepped into her drab but official office.

"Prudie Zimmer, it's my pleasure to introduce you to Captain Ash Kennett. It was his crew that did the deed."

"Well, hello there, you handsome man," she said, giving Ash a hug, which caught him off guard.

"Remember the fight at Zula Thunder," the beaming Swain went on as if this was a regular occurrence?

"Of course, I do," Mrs. Zimmer said, stepping back. "Saved our asses in the last war."

"Ash here and a couple of his crew earned CMVs in that battle. "

"A real honest to God hero," Prudie said.

"There are 22,000 souls who I believe would argue with that title."

"That you have not forgotten them says a lot for you, Captain. Anything you want or need, just name it. Tell anybody who asks that Prudie said it was a command."

"That's — more than — generous," Ash said, getting his breath back. "Thank you, Station Master."

"It's Prudie to you, Captain. I have the whole story in a report from Elwood," she gestured to her oversized holistic display above her desk. "This so-called Captain Percival Randsom was nothing more than a petty thief and racketeer who got lucky and stole a ship. He's a want-to-be pirate — but you took care of that pretty damn quickly," she laughed as she motioned both her guests to chairs, and she took the center seat of the couch.

Ash didn't know exactly what happened to criminals. Different corporations had their unique way of dealing with such scum. The felon class was of absolutely no value to any corporation. And if there was no bottom line advantage, they had their solutions. From hard labor, which was almost as expensive to support as incarceration, to complete mind wiping to summary execution, there was little future for criminals.

"The ship's original name was THE PESTILENCE," Captain Swain said, but I think I'll rename her THE JANICE LOUISE — sister to THE BETTY RUTH. How'd ya' like it?"

"Sounds good to me. I'd sail on her."

"Any time, Captain. Once I get her through the shipyards and rebuild her as a passenger cruiser, you and your crew are all welcome aboard any time."

"Then I'll see you around the shipyards, Captain Swain. I'm here to pick up my new ship — THE ERRANT. Either you or the shipyard will have to navigate her to her rebuild site. With Mrs. — Prudie's permission, THE PESTILENCE is yours to move."

"There is the matter of changing ownership," the Station Master reminded them. She opened a folder and pushed it across her desk to the two men. "Both of you sign here and here. You'll have to get her name changed at the shipyards."

They both signed, shook hands, and Prudie wanted another hug, which Ash gladly obliged.

"Let's make a point of breaking bread a couple of times while both of you are here," she said, releasing Ash with a smile.

"Name the time and place," Ash said. "I'll be there."

"I never say no to a free meal,' Captain Swain laughed.

~

PRUDIE HAD a message waiting for Ash. She handed it to him when he left the Station Master's office. It was from Doc Eugene. All it said was, "Call me."

Ash blinked on the message icon in his heads-up display, and his friend picked up.

"How'd you even know I was here?" Ash asked.

"Your NCOIC — Birgitta Perry — she's on the job every second. Called me the moment you docked your new prize. She sent your kit over, and it's already here. Take the elevator up three decks. It'll bring you right to me. Come meet your new ship."

Ash couldn't help but shake his head and smile

at SMC Perry's efficiency. Ash didn't know what the procedures would be with the pirate craft and hadn't bothered to pick up any of his few belongings before heading to the Station Master's office. Now he had Doc's invitation.

"I'm on my way," he said to Doc.

"While you're coming, tell me about your mining claim. Did you get what you wanted for it?"

"In a way."

"Explain."

"Remember the guy who hit me over the back with the plastisteel chair in the bar fight?"

"The one you put to sleep with a fist in the face?"

"That's him. I sold it to him — on terms?"

Ash talked as he took the elevator to the level where Doc awaited him.

"Glover Rowtag. Family name is Algonquian — native American from a century or two ago."

"He must have some family stories."

"You don't want to get him started. Well, maybe you do — but I made that mistake once. I ended up so drunk it took me a week to recover. Anyway, his and three sons bought my claim — only they couldn't afford it. So, I kept a 1/3 ownership and gave him terms he could meet to pay off the rest. I also have first dibs on all the disco-lite I might ever need — at whatever the current market price is."

"So, a win-win?"

"I thought so. Glover and his boys, their wives, and children are good people — all they've ever needed was a break. The claim they were working was keeping them housed and fed but not much else. Now, they can have a better life. And they'll work at it."

"I do want to meet these people."

"Well, I'm on deck four. Which way?"

"Take the arm in front of you out to the yard docks. You'll see her as soon as you step out. She's in the first dock on the right."

CHAPTER TWENTY

The dock was sealed off from the outside. All the station's berths were on the outside of the spinning port rings. This produced artificial gravity making all activity on the docks much easier. Tugs had to maneuver each arriving or departing vessel in and out.

To say THE ERRANT was gigantic was to underestimate the size of a cruiser spacecraft. She was nineteen stories high and longer than 3 of the largest ocean-going container ships of about 460 meters each. She measured out at over 1,370 meters. Ash could not help but convert it to feet in his head. He came up with 3,500 feet.

As Ash looked up at the massive carrier, he marveled at the structure. It was modular with jutting antennas, dishes as well as a raised command tower towards the rear. Ash walked the full length of the craft until he could see the 12 rear varying size propulsion openings and one large port he assumed was for the FTL drive.

"Think she'll do?" Doc asked. He had been there when Ash first approached THE ERRANT but seeing how the new captain was awestruck, Doc stayed silent and walked behind as Ash inspected the ship.

"Damn," Ash said, realizing Doc was now beside him, "my last cruiser wasn't this massive."

"You know the Crux Corporation — they loved to spend money, and they liked building huge. Only the Hudson-Sturdivant out sized them. And that was only in the battleship class. Their damn T-rex was truly called 'a terror.'"

"And this is the smallest of the Crux carriers? I never came across them in battle."

"That's what they say. Come on. Let me show you the interior of this small Crux carrier."

∾

Doc, still wearing his brown robes, led Ash through THE ERRANT. She had two empty hanger bays and a third with a shuttle, and six predatory Scorpion fighters.

"See, we have an additional fighter," Doc said.

"Where do these things come from?"

"Two came from collectors who died, one from a museum which already had two that were junkers — and the last we made ourselves."

"How did you make them?"

"You didn't notice the last hanger? It's a massive 3D printer. We can make more fighters if we want, or any replacement parts."

"But all these six are in fighting shape?"

"Better than before. From one collector, we got the factory specs and blueprints."

It took Ash a moment to absorb all of this. He shook his head slowly in amazement.

Center below decks was a double football field ecosystem with hydroponics, dirt growing vegetables, and fruit trees. Grass, vines, and live chickens thrived in the light and temperature-controlled space. There was an additional section for healing plants like aloe vera, milk thistle, and chamomile.

The bottom most deck, which of course they did not visit, was the massively external shielded artificial gravity producing and constantly boiling magma.

Sickbay had a half dozen auto-docs and, in a separate room, an operating table. A halo MRI sat at the head of the slab, which was flanked by robot surgery units.

Doc was most pleased with the kitchen and mess. Shiney and gleaming, a cafeteria serving line and three coffee urns were close by the door. Back in the kitchen, one wall was replete with multiple cold storage units, and at a right angle, a stovetop with a multiplex of heating surfaces. Mixers, choppers, and food containers were mounted to the table.

Ash was very pleased with the comfort and space allowed in every living quarter.

But it was the bridge that the new Captain wanted to see most. The Captain's ready room was ahead of the vessel's control space while CIC was behind. All were shielded deep inside the ship. Large and colorful screens were at each station, navigation, weapons, and communications. The Captain's chair was raised on a platform with a second chair beside it for an executive officer.

The ship's interior colors were deep purple, grey, and white. It sparkled and even smelled factory new.

"What do you think, El Capitain?"

"I'm pleased and very impressed. It lives up to

everything you told me — and more. Now we need to complete her crew and take her out for a test run."

"One more improvement you need to know about, Ash, it has the ability to cloak."

"That's been the dream but no one's been able to pull it off, yet."

"You need to meet the genius who made all of this happen."

SANTANA VANDERHOOF STOOD with his legs apart, shoulders back and a frown on his elongated face sporting bushy eyebrows on his protruding brow. His beefy body was made even larger by the meaty fists planted on his hips. Genetics had paused his age at 52.

"Do you want to bet your life on that capsule?" he scorned a drawing displayed on a projection drawing table.

A young woman, attractive features, brown hair curled under at her shoulders, held a palm-sized tablet in her petite hands. She held her ground beside the larger man, examining the tilted line drawing on the table.

"Check the framing — the exoskeleton — and

the energy displacement under-skin. And yes, I would bet my life on it." Leggy and slender, she looked in her twenties but was actually in her mid-thirties. She held her ground with the strength of will.

"You've stress-tested it?"

The look she gave the older man would wilt anyone not as commanding as he.

"I don't show you anything unless it's ready — father."

He zoomed in on the specs and then back out to the entire capsule.

"I want to see a model."

"It's being printed as you waste my time here."

A knuckle tapped on the Yardmaster's door.

Santana turned to see Doc and his companion in the door frame.

The shipbuilder strode over and offered his hand to Ash. "The man of the hour."

"Master Vanderhoof," Ash took the man's hand.

"Captain," the man said. "But if we're going to be partners, I'd prefer to be on a first-name basis. I'm Santana."

"Ash."

"And I'm still Doc if anybody cares," Doc said with a grin.

"We've seen your face so much I see it when I can't sleep," Vanderhoof said. "And this is my daughter," the Yardmaster said, gesturing the young woman forward, "Starla — Dr. times two — Vanderhoof. Ph.D. in spacecraft propulsion and one in design."

"Let's not start comparing doctorates," she said, stepping up to the group and offering her hand to Ash. "I'm sure Doc will win with a few degrees tied behind him."

"Am I that obvious," Doc smiled.

"You are, Doc," Ash said. "And we all know it." He shook hands with the young woman, and they all laughed -- even Doc.

"Such friends," he said.

"Starla was the project head for THE ER-RANT," her father said proudly. "Most of your in-ovations come from her — especially your cloaking and your improved FTL engines. She owns the patents."

"From what I've seen on a quick walkthrough, I confess I am dazzled. Can't wait to take her out."

"You talking about the ship or my daughter," Santana said with a wink.

"Father — really?" Starla was blushing.

Doc changed the subject as he turned to Ash, "How's the staffing and crewing coming along?"

"Fairly well. We should meet a few more prospects here."

"I just had a brilliant idea," Santana said.

"Should we take cover?" Doc asked.

"Do you have a chief engineer yet?"

"No."

"I'd like to suggest my daughter. Starla, what do you think?"

"Engineer? Me?" The suggestion came out of galactic orbit for her.

"Nobody knows this ship better than you do."

"But I'm not military?"

"You were Corporation ROTC until you dropped out to go to grad school — the first time," her father said.

"I'm not commissioned."

"I believe I can take care of that," Ash said.

"But an ensign as Engineering Chief?" Starla asked.

"What's say we make it, Lieutenant — Commander?"

"Lieutenant Commander?" Starla asked.

"Seems fair to me. Two doctorates. What do you think, Doc?"

"You could use the experience," her father said.

"All three partners agree," Doc smiled.

"Are you sure, Captain?" she asked.

"We'd be lucky and honored."

Starla stuck out her hand again. "You've got yourself an engineering chief. When do I report?"

"Tomorrow, 09:00 local time."

"What's the uniform?"

"Perhaps you could check on that. My NCOIC will know. Senior Master Chief Birgitta Perry. They call her the Briquet. When you meet her, you'll understand. I'll have her contact you."

CHAPTER TWENTY-ONE

Bartholomew Lutz exploded into a rage that came near to a conflagration when Arluna Ito burst into the middle of a session Lutz was having with Jaxlynn Shellanberger. He forced the young woman off of him and fury overtook him as the second in command brought him the news of THE PESTILENCE's capture.

The naked pirate king cared nothing for Captain Percival Randsom or his crew. Lutz shouted in his penetrating voice, "How did this happen?"

"He attacked a target of opportunity, a loaded cargo hauler called THE BETTY RUTH."

"I don't care what it was called!" Lutz bellowed. "He was supposed to deliver slaves! Nothing more!"

"According to the reports, he had no slaves onboard. They must have been delivered," Ito said not noticing Jaxlynn on the floor beside the sprawling bed.

Lutz gold nose ring swung as he stalked the room. "He and his crew were taken alive?"

"Correct. Well, Randsom and others were killed."

"Then somebody will talk. Do you know what this means, Arluna?"

"We are vulnerable! We can be found."

"Let's not get ahead of ourselves. This was a one off."

"How did it happen? THE PESTILENCE out-gunned any cargo carrier?"

"The report says, " Arluna said reading from her tablet, "the cargo vessel covered '... the pirate ship with landing foam, including its engine ports. The ship was dead in space — unable to move.'"

"And who fought our men?"

Again Arluna consulted her tablet. "A company of security officers led by Captain Ash Kennett, CMV, captured the boarding party and took over the attacking ship."

Jaxlynn had to cup both hands over her mouth to keep from screaming in delight.

"'The former PESTILENCE,'" Arluna read, "'was taken to shipyards at Xanadu Transit above planet Tatius's Luna Nineteen."

"I know who Ash Kennett is. That son-of-a-bitch! I killed his slut of a wife with that cargo drone when we took out that government lacky who didn't pay up when he was due."

"THE PESTILENCE is being refitted and re-named," Arluna said.

"And where is Ash Kennett?"

"There I suppose. The report doesn't say. Are we going after him?"

"Hell no! Not now — not yet. If Kennett has a security company — what else does he have? Ships — armored ships — battle ships?" Lutz wandered the room a minute before he looked up at Arluna. "Let's get some active satellites up and far out. If they're coming for us, I want to know it. We need to beef up our planet defenses — put all ships on alert."

It was then that Lutz noticed Jaxlynn. He stopped and shouted at her, "Get out!!"

She fled the room using a huge sheet to cover herself. Her modesty wasn't as much a concern for her as the smile and joy which was swelling inside her. She didn't want any of the guards or others in the harem to be aware of her delight.

~

THERE WAS HOPE, but Jaxlynn knew she had no one to share it with. Or was there?

Roaming through the pirate's computer system with her tablet Jaxlynn had discovered three other uncharted footprints. She followed them and tracked them to a farm, a warehouse, and the labor slave market. All three had been going to the same sites Jaxlynn had visited — communications, ground defense, and the orbiting spaceport above Deadwood. Although she could not put a name, much less a face, to any of the three, she was convinced that these were people with computer knowledge from their tracks. They also appeared to share a longing for freedom and even the destruction of the pirate world.

Now that she had news that was hope, she sent a message to the three. It read: "You are not invisible. Add this to your front porch." She then added a piece of computer code designed to mask entries on the "front porch" or the first line of any entry into the system.

As soon as she did, each signal went dead. She could only imagine the coders' reaction who abruptly got such a message on what they must have believed to be undetectable tracks. They would be startled and sat back in shock. As they read the line of code Jaxlynn offered and even carefully studied it, they would realize it did cover their online work. But each must have been so rattled that they disconnected from the network and did not attempt to reconnect for several days. They'd have been waiting to be arrested and killed.

When nothing happened, the three must have gone back on line very carefully — attaching the suggested line of code — and discovered they could go anywhere on the net and be as undetectable as they had thought before. It took a week for all three to be back online, each still ignorant of the others. Jaxlynn gave them a few days before she contacted them individually. Unknown to them, the code provided the anonymity they sought and made them instantly recognizable to her. The next message was — "There is reason for hope. Do not give up."

Then another week went by before Jaxlynn requested an online meeting on a never used recycling node. At the prearranged time, she told them about THE PESTILENCE capture and Bartholomew Lutz's fear that Deadwood could now be found. She still kept the three separate from each other, thinking that only they and whoever Jaxlynn was were involved in the secret sharing of info on the web.

What surprised Jaxlynn was that soon each of the others were sharing information about that status of operation within their knowledge. They each assured her that there were many who would join in a take over of the planet of Deadwood when such a time arrived.

CHAPTER TWENTY-TWO

"Is this the *'round table'*?" Ash asked as the trio of THE ERRANT owners sat down around a small plastisteel table in the Yardmaster's Office.

Santana Vanderhoof looked across at Doc and they shared a laugh.

"It is," Doc said. "Not very impressive is it?"

"Everything has to start somewhere," Ash said. "Perhaps my news will be well met. We already have an income." He explained about THE BETTY RUTH's owner's generosity. "We have Captain's shares for each of us of 40% of the new craft's income. THE PESTILENCE will be called THE JANICE LOUISE. The crew who helped save her also get their allotted parts of the shares,"

Ash told them. "The former THE WICKED WAYS is now the second in the fleet of Captain Elwood Swain." They toasted the omen of marvelous adventures ahead.

~

A SUITE of rooms at Xanadu Transit's Hotel Nebula continued to be used for screening potential staff and crew. A black coverall wearing spacer directed applicants to the correct interview room.

SMC Birgitta Perry approached Ash in the main room during a break. Ash asked about uniforms.

"Petty Officer Wyatt Light — our dog robber — has been on it, Sir."

"Did you give a status report on the project to our new Chief Engineer?"

"I did, Sir. Light has two Able Spacers on it. One was a vid customer before the war and the other a former theatre major in college. I talked to them and explained you wanted something understated, unique, and practical."

"Exactly. How did you know that?"

"It appears to be your tastes, Sir."

"Then I'll just leave it in their hands."

"We should have something this week, Sir."

~

THE DOOR OPENED to the Officer Core inter-viewing room, where Ash and two other officers waited. The woman who entered was stout with erect posture, professionally cut brown-streaked blonde hair, and an oval face. Her small mouth opened in surprise when she spotted Ash. She closed her mouth and executed an about-face before halting in place at the calling of her name.

"Commander Olin!" Ash called. "Beula Olin," he got to his feet behind the table.

The olive-skinned woman, dressed in pants and a matching dark blue high collared blouse, stopped and slowly turned around to see Ash ap-proaching. "If I'd known this was your operation, Captain, I wouldn't have wasted either of our time."

"You've not wasted mine," Ash said with a pleasant smile. "I didn't want my name associated with the advertisement, especially because I hoped you might show up."

The remark took her aback.

"Why?" the middle 30s looking woman questioned but did not move from her place in the doorway.

"I wanted to offer you a position."

"No, thank you," she said and started to go once more. "I don't work with addicts."

"You've come this far. What will it hurt to hear me out? You can always say no again — and even slap me in the face if that helps."

"Captain, you have no idea how tempting that possibility is."

"I can imagine," Ash said. "Let's go next door for a little privacy."

She took a breath and sighed before deciding, "What the hell?"

The vacant room they entered was a hotel bedroom. She gave Ash her most damning expression. He crossed to the table and took one chair, motioning to another for her. Reluctantly, she took the seat.

"What are you doing these days, Beula?"

"Commanding my own ship."

"An ore collector to the asteroid belt and back? An over sized space going pickup truck." He managed to say this without the insult the words could have held.

"I'm content," she said after allowing herself a moment to recompose herself.

"Are you? Then why did you come here?"

She didn't answer the question. Instead, she stated the obvious, "You and I are oil and seaweed. We don't mix — we don't fit — we don't work together."

"We did once."

"Is that the way you remember it? What I recall is an obstinate man who trusted his gut over the council of those around him. Even -- and especially when he was drunk."

"Not always."

"Let's say 80% of the time."

"I'd give you 60% — but not eighty. I thought we worked well together."

"How could you possibly conclude that?"

"You were such a detail person — perfectionist — by the book — logical — thoughtful — and you argued your positions effectively. Believe it or not, Beula, you were the best officer I ever served with."

"Don't make me gag."

"No, it's true. What do you expect from your Executive Officer?"

"I don't have one."

"Let's suppose you did. What would you consider to be their duties?"

She tightened and then relaxed her jaw. "To

keep the ship in order, on schedule, disciplined — and to offer suggestions when the occasion demanded."

"Perhaps you didn't know it, but part of an XO's job was to disagree with the captain — even challenge him or her. Sometimes its being a devil's advocate and taking the polar opposite position -- and to argue it. I know I'm a big picture guy. You're a minute, point by point — sometimes even a micromanagement person."

"Sometimes?" She did laugh this time, but it had no humor to it.

"What kind of command do you have now? I understand it's not that big, but you're a god in your way. I'll bet you have a troop of yes-men who never dare challenge you?"

Her mouth tightened at this image.

"You don't need that. You are too focused and deliberative. What do you do when the book is wrong — when the rules don't work?"

"I don't allow that to happen."

"It does in combat."

Silence settled between the two for several moments.

"You are on the wagon?"

Ash nodded.

"How long?"

"Three years. And forever — I hope."

"You hope? And if you slip — how many people will die?"

"I can't promise forever — only yesterday and today. Too many have died already. That's what started me down that path. I'm off of it now."

"Being a captain means you are going to have to order people into harms way."

"That's what has taken me a couple of years to sort out. I hate that part of it. But it comes with the job. What I want is an Exec with the knowledge and the backbone to call me on my rash decisions — to kick me in the ass when I need it. And the strength to take over if I'm a danger to the ship."

Beula Olin had been a Lt. Commander under Ash in the last war. They would never be friends — but they were a balance Ash knew he needed.

"I almost did exactly that a couple of times during the war — but even drunk you were an amazing tactician.

"Let explain me this job before you say no — or slap me for good measure."

"I'm listening," she finally said.

"We have an abandoned Crux carrier — used to be one of their smallest. It's been completely redone. Ostensively we will be cargo haulers —

but we have, at the moment, six Scorpion fighters, and we'll have a dozen within the month. They're all new and refitted and upgraded — just like THE ERRANT."

"THE ERRANT."

"She is still fully armed — although disguised — with, I'm told, FTL capabilities nobody else has. Plus cloaking."

"Real cloaking that works?"

"I thought that might get your attention. We will also have a crew of warriors — if you've ever seen the old vid, we are Fighting Seabees. We are going pirate hunting — Bartholomew Lutz, to be exact. And eventually, when this war is over, we'll leave a few ships on patrol on this end of the galaxy. We're going out to the Delporte quadrant."

"That's the other end of the galaxy."

"That's what I said. But according to Doc — Doc Bywater — you remember him?"

"Doc? Bywater?"

"He found the ship and dreamed this all up in the three years it took him to get the ship here."

"Why didn't you lead with that? I love Doc. Him I trust."

"We're all in this together. We'd very much like to include you."

"What's the rest of it? What's at the other end of the galaxy."

"A minor planet out there named Camlann. We plan to involve ourselves in its war."

"As mercs?"

"I'm not sure what we'll be — but it will be right, or we won't do it. Everyone on board will have a vote. We are free agents and pick our fights. It's a hell of a lot more fun than collecting helium — and a better use of your talents. Doc convinced me I'm a warrior, and that's the kind of people we're looking for. Warriors who are good people — we're going to be the 'few good men' — and women — who will stand up to those in the wrong."

Beula studied Ash a minute and stood. She paced the floor another half minute and came back to the table. Ash stood awaiting her answer.

"I'll accept — one minute from now."

Ash wrinkled his forehead. He offered her his hand. "Welcome aboard, Commander."

Before she accepted it, she said, "If I even suspect you're off the wagon, I'll relieve you of command on the spot — and pronounce it a mutanty"

"I would expect nothing less. Okay?" he asked slowly.

Then Beula slapped Ash's left cheek so hard it

turned his head. He looked back at his soon-to-be executive officer rubbing his face and flexing his jaw. He said, "Beula, for you, I'll even turn the other cheek."

"Not necessary," she said with a wicked grin. "But it had to be done."

They shook hands.

CHAPTER TWENTY-THREE

In a month, THE ERRANT was up to its new strength level of 512 souls. Included were the support ranks of maintenance and stewards. The support departments were Medical, Supply, and Maintenance. The command departments were Aviation, Engineering, Navigation, Tactical, and Weapons. A Lt. Commander headed each. The Scorpions flight leader's title was the CSF (Commander Starship Fighter). But tradition kept the old blue water navy term, CAG which meant Commander Air Group. Starla Vanderhoof was Chief Engineer. Navigation handled course calculations at both normal and Faster Than Light (FTL) travel. Tactical comprised Intelligence, Meteorology, and Electronics, which included all communications and Ground Combat Direction. The Weapons Department crewed the multi-rail guns, lasers, torpedoes, missiles, and point defense systems, as well as defense countermeasures.

Beyond all these functions, the crew maintained the facade of cargo handling. Ash felt they were almost ready for their shake down cruise.

EVERY MEMBER of the crew had to be checked through an autodoc before being officially accepted aboard THE ERRANT. The unit recorded their vitals, including uniform size requirements. As the ship's crew grew, each spacer, NCO and officer were assigned living quarters and work stations when they boarded. By the end of their first day, every crew member was delivered a set of uniforms.

The new uniforms were black boots, pants, and a blouse with a diagonal purple stripe 4 inches wide across the chest. The band collars all had a two-inch opening in the center. There was a silver piping stripe down the legs of the officer's uniforms.

All uniforms had the words "THE ERRANT"

stitched on the end of their shoulder boards. A black beret was stowed on the right shoulder-board, and gloves on the left.

The uniforms' cloth seemed to breathe, but in a lack of atmosphere, it changed to airtight. The pants sealed to the boots, and a mask could be pulled from the beret which was see-through but airtight and sealed to the collar. The gloves, too, sealed when worn. The uniform contained an hour's worth of oxygen, enabling the wearer to have an unarmored EVA suit.

Enlisted ranks began with a stitched comet one inch from the end of each sleeve. One 1/2 inch vertical stripe indicated a basic Spacer Recruit. Two stripes were for an Apprentice Spacer, and three showed an Able Spacer.

Identical horizontal bands could top the stripes — one for Petty Officer Third Class, two for Petty Officer Second Class, and three for Petty Officer First Class. One diamond above the stripes was for Chief Petty Officer, two diamonds for Master Chief Petty Officer, and three for Senior Master Chief. Only the Briquet, Birgitta Perry, had four diamonds in a pyramid. This stood for her position as Command Senior Master Chief, the NCOIC (Noncommissioned Officer In Charge).

Officer ranks were worn on their collars. An open silver triangle for an ensign, a solid silver triangle for a lieutenant junior grade, and two solid silver triangles for a lieutenant. An open four-pointed gold star was for a Lieutenant Commander, and a solid gold four-pointed star was for a Commander. Two solid four-pointed stars were for the Captain.

Every crew member had a set of class A uniforms and a set of dress whites as well. Additionally, fatigues were black and purple, which had subdued rank insignias. These uniforms were composed of a material that could convert to an invisible cloaked suit. Again the cap, gloves, and pants sealed when required.

Ash was so pleased with the uniforms that he had the creators promoted to Petty Officer 1st class.

❧

THE ERRANT LIVED up to exceptions. Ash and his XO, Commander Beula Olin, took turns testing every system, even going slightly above its prescribed limits.

Every department and function of the ship were tested and retested. Drills were organized from full battle stations to response to possible accidents. Enthusiasm was high as all on board took pride in being the first to examine and tryout every function. At meals they bragged to each other about how this was the best ship they have ever served on.

Both Ash and Buela kept coming up with emergencies and combat conditions to stress both the crew and the ship. Ash began a program of cross training all the officer and crew members on the functions and duties of others onboard. Spacers were put into a sealed compartment with no lights and taught to find knobs and levers in total darkness of each compartment.

One day Commander Olin said to Ash as he came on duty a few minutes early as was his custom, "Captain, your Chief Engineer has requested a private meeting with you. She said it should not take more than twenty minutes."

"Ask her to meet me in the conference room," Ash said. "I should be able to relieve you on schedule, XO."

"Aye, aye, Sir."

Ash left the bridge for the conference room as Commander Olin contacted Lt. Commander Vanderhoof.

~

ASH SEARCHED in the unfamiliar galaxy outside the conference room's port hole for any patterns like the type of constellations he'd known in other galaxies — but he found none.

A chime sounded. Without turning, he said, "Come!"

The door swished open, and Lt. Commander Starla Vanderhoof entered. She came to attention and saluted.

"Thank you for seeing me, Captain."

Ash turned and was struck by the sight of the young woman resplendent in her uniform. It took him a moment to return her salute and offer her a seat. They both sat on the side of the table nearest the door.

"What can I do for you, Commander?" he asked.

"I believe I've made a breakthrough, Captain."

"What kind of breakthrough?"

"Will you close your eyes, Sir?"

He complied.

"I believe I've discovered a novel way we can communicate." Her voice changed as she said, "*If I'm correct, it will be a significant advance — one we should keep to ourselves.*"

"*How is she doing this?*" Ash's AI asked inside his head.

"*Doing what?*" Ash quarried his AI.

"*Speaking to you inside your head. Look at her,*" Zulli spoke again .

Ash opened his eyes and saw Lt. Commander Vanderhoof sitting there with her mouth closed.

"Did your AI speak to you, Captain?"

"How do you know that?"

Still, without moving her lips, she spoke in his head. "*I've found a way to communicate from internal nerolink to nerolink. While your AI can hear me, without your permission, I can't talk to or hear her.*"

Ash stared at Vanderhoof. Then inside his head, he asked, "*Can you hear me now?*"

"*Yes, Sir, I can. May I speak to your AI?*"

"*Zulli, can you hear Commander Vanderhoof?*"

"*You mean Lt. Commander Vanderhoof?*"

"*Of course. Speak to her.*"

"*How about 'kiss my ass, Lt. Commander'?*"

"I don't believe you have one," Vanderhoof smiled at Captain Kennett.

"*I think she's right, Zulli.*"

"*Does that mean you'd like her to kiss yours?*"

"*Zulli!*"

Starla laughed out loud.

"How did you manage this?" Ash asked. "Zulli's a chip inside my head."

"And Phaedra, my AI, is mine." *"Say hello, Phaedra."*

"Hello, Zulli. You're the first AI in someone else's head I've ever talked to."

"This is very strange to me — but I think I could get used to it," Zulli said.

"All our AI's have their frequency," the Lt. Commander explained. "Most of them work on only a few frequencies. With a little work, I was able to create a network between us. We could do this for the entire ship and have independent networks within networks if needed. You and I, for example, could talk to each other while still being able to talk to anyone on the ship."

"That's absolutely amazing. Does it have to be line-of-sight? How far can it reach?"

"Distance I'm not sure of, yet, but it doesn't have to be line-of-sight. As long as we've given the nerolinks permission or an individual permission, we can speak neruolink to neruolink."

"How close are you to perfecting this?"

"Pretty close, Captain. But I didn't want to continue it without your permission."

"Permission granted, Commander. Please keep me abreast of your progress.

"Aye, aye, Sir."

CHAPTER TWENTY-FOUR

During the last planned week of THE ERRANT's shakedown cruise, it received an SOS signal from a distant freighter under attack by pirates.

"How long would it take to get us there, Commander Shrer?" Ash asked the officer standing next to the lieutenant seated at the Navigation station. The second half of THE ERRANT's Scorpion starfighter were out on a check flight at that moment.

After a quick calculation, the square-jawed Shrer said, "If our FTL engines perform as tested, about a quarter of an hour."

"Plot a course," Ash said as he tapped a button on one of his command chair's arms. "Engineer, secure from impulse power. Stand by to jump to FTL. See the plot from Navigation. Recover all Scorpions immediately!"

"Are you sure of this, Captain," XO Olin quietly asked from her chair beside Ash.

He opened his mouth and breathed out for her.

She sniffed and acknowledged his command with a nod.

Within two minutes, all the fighters were back aboard. To the crew Ash announced, "Battle stations!" To Engineering he ordered, "Secure for impulse. Prepare to jump to FTL."

"Aye, aye, Sir," came the response.

Pressing another button, the Captain ordered, "Weapons, prepare to engage cloaking." To a third department, he said, "CSF, keep pilots in recovered squadron of Scorpions in their fighters!" Finally, he contacted Tactical. "Lt. Commander Blunie, prepare four boarding teams."

"Aye, aye," came the response from each department.

ONE-QUARTER OF AN HOUR LATER, THE ERRANT took up station under and perpendicular to a water hauler. THE ERRANT also stretched beyond the vessels on either side of the cargo ship.

To his bridge crew, Ash commanded, "Full scan of all three ships. Open a channel to the Captain of — ."

"THE JACK AND JILL," came the information from Intelligence in the combat information center (CIC). "The Captain's name is Nona Laflin."

"Channel open, Captain," said Lt. J.G. Georgeanna Kinnaman. The bright-eyed, ash gray-haired young Comms Officer was efficient to the point of almost expecting each of Ash's commands.

"Captain Laflin, this is Captain Ash Kennett of THE ERRANT. We are here to assist you. Can you speak freely?"

"Yes," came the reply in a questioning tone. "Who are you, and where are you?"

"We are directly beneath you — cloaked but very capable of dealing with your adversaries." Ash looked at the scanning images he'd called up on his personal screen beside his chair. "We see pirates setting charges to blow your bridge doors and others still in two of your airlocks. Do you have hull breach patches handy and bots to use them on your lowest and top decks?"

It took a moment for the hauler's Captain to process all she was being told and asked. When she responded, she said, "Affirmative."

"We can see that your shields are down to five percent. Can you cope with them completely down on my count?"

"Well," Captain Laflin said, "They're almost useless to us."

"On the count of three. Weapons," Ash said, "drop cloaking and use our topside mini railguns to take out those in the hallway outside the bridge.

"Aye, aye, Captain."

"Three, two, one. Execute!"

The freighter's shields dropped, as did those of THE ERRANT. Five precision mini railgun shots penetrated THE JACK AND JILL from its lower hull and out the top of the ship. Along the way, the shots passed through all five pirates. They fell dead like bags of seed dropping to the deck.

"Shields up,"" Ash ordered.

Captain Laflin ordered her damage control bots to the breaches with hull sealing patches.

THE ERRANT was now visible to both pirate ships.

Ash asked, "Captain Laflin. How many crew do you have, and where are they?"

"Twenty-three. They are sheltered in place."

"The pirate ships have targeted us, Captain," came a voice from CIC. "But they haven't gotten a lock yet thanks to our stealth shielding."

"Weapons, target and disable their shields. Then take out the umbilicals from both pirate ships. Captain Laflin, please keep your intruders confined to your airlocks. Comms, hail both pirate vessels."

There were two beeps, and the startled voices of the two pirate commanders shouted, "Who the hell is this?"

"Captain Ash Kennett of THE ERRANT. Surrender immediately or," he paused before saying slowly, "'to dust you will return.'"

The ship on the far side of the hauler was a near antique corvette. It had been poorly maintained but was sufficiently threatening to an unarmed freighter like THE JACK AND JILL. On its port side was a craft that had once been a battle cruiser — now neglected but armed with missiles nearing a century of service. This was the larger of the two ships.

"We have you targeted!" one of the pirate captains shouted.

"No, he doesn't," CIC assured Ash.

"You are only microseconds from your death. Surrender. I will not ask again," Ash responded.

"The corvette has its guns on line and is firing on us, Captain," Intelligence said from CIC.

THE ERRANT shook from the impact of multiple point blank shots from the corvette.

"Weapons, take out the corvette!" Ash ordered.

In an instant, the old ship was debris flaming from its escaping internal atmosphere before it was the black center of hurling shrapnel — then nothing.

"Damage report!"

"Forward hull breach on decks two, eight, and seven. Impacts on decks five and twenty. Five killed, multiple injuries."

"The cruiser is powering down, Captain," came the announcement from CIC.

"Get the injured to sickbay!" Ash commanded.

"Commander Beula Olin, "Seal off the breached compartments! Dispatch droids to patch the breaches!"

Ash's next order went out to the bridge but also over the channel open to the remaining pirate ship. "Tactical, dispatch boarding parties to the other ship with orders to kill at the slightest resistance." He turned to Olin. "Why did the corvette's shots get through our shields?"

"Because we were too close. It was partly inside our shields, Captain."

Ash felt like a fool. Crew members were dead because of his decision. His XO was right in her warning — because the navigator had plotted a course too close to THE JACK AND JILL. But Ash didn't blame the navigator. The responsibility was his and his alone.

CHAPTER TWENTY-FIVE

Ash and Doc appeared for dinner aboard THE JACK AND JILL as requested. They wore their dress whites.

They were welcomed aboard by Captain Nona Laflin, a woman who appeared to be 50, salt and pepper hair, sharp cheekbones and a heavy-set body.

They were treated to a delicious feast of venison and fresh vegetables at a table with three other JACK AND JILL officers.

"You set a fine table," Doc said. He dressed in a commander's uniform.

"That and good pay keeps my people coming back," Captain Laflin said.

"Will you consider it bad manners, Captain

Kennett, to discuss your business? I'd like to know about it — and how much we owe you for your intervention in our moment of distress."

"No charge," Ash said.

"Are you sure? I will contribute my captain's share from the haul."

"And mine," said another of THE JACK AND JILL's officers.

"It's unnecessary. We are on our shakedown cruise. I consider this incident a training exercise."

"Plus, we are claiming the cruiser as our prize," Doc added.

"You're welcome to it with my blessing. Please allow me to record an endorsement for your records."

"That would be helpful," Ash agreed.

"Is bounty hunting your business?"

"I never thought of it that way," Doc said. "But I should have."

"We are ostensibly in the freight business, too," Ash said. "But our true mission is commercial security."

"Do you have clients?"

"Not, yet."

"Because," she said, "we independent haulers

like THE JACK AND JILL could never afford your service."

"But you could if you banded together with other independents?" Doc offered.

"Banding together is against our nature, Commander," Captain Laflin said. "That's why we're independent."

"I understand," Ash said. "I was an independent miner for a few years. I understand the need to be free."

"But," Doc said, "there is strength in numbers. What you can't afford, a group of freighters with nothing beyond security in common could easily handle. No need to unionize or to share any trade secrets or clients. Stay independent but contribute a little to security. What no one of you could afford individually for an incident such as this could be simply a small cost of doing business. Less than the lowest crew's quarter share of each trip. Certainly cheaper than losing everything."

"Your combined information about pirate encounters could also help us build a database with which we could crush this menace for good," Ash finished.

Captain Laflin sat back and considered the concept. After a few moments of thought, she said, "Let me contact some other captains — and owners. You might have come up with a dynamic solution to a problem we all face."

"I'VE ASSIGNED a prize crew to THE WICKED WAYS," XO Olin told Ash as soon as he and Doc returned from THE JACK AND JILL.

"That's her name? THE WICKED WAYS?"

"It is. I put Lt. Commander Talmage from Supply in charge of the detail. Ensign Javon Haygood said he piloted THE PESTILENCE for you, so I detached him to be the pilot. I made Petty Officer Miguel Cyril NCOIC and also assigned his fully armed team for on-board security."

"Excellent," Ash said. "But you may want to head this prize crew, XO."

"Why's that, Captain?"

"Because she's going to be your new ship."

THE ERRANT MADE few appearances at space stations except to pick up or discharge cargo. This kept up the facade of her being a cargo ship.

However, her primary business was pirate hunting.

The independent cargo haulers banded together and were clients of Round Table Venture. Business was good.

THE ERRANT captured seven vessels, redeeming all but two for their recovery bounty. The odd two vessels were sent to the Xanadu Transit shipyard to be refitted, rearmed, and rechristened.

First was a Taxexa Corporation cruiser captured as THE WICKED WAYS. Beula Olin gladly accepted the promotion to Captain and command of the new vessel. She renamed it THE GREEN NIGHT. Taxexa made communications equipment before the war and had a fleet of sleek, fast cruisers to transport components and finished products. They made an excellent ship.

Commander Olin took command of the refitted ships and asked, with Ash's approval, for three officers, seven NCOs to go with her from THE ERRANT. She had to recruit the rest of her officers and crew. The task was made easier because the Corporations were trying to get out of the military business. Three Scorpions were given to THE GREEN NIGHT, along with a 3D printer capable of making their own force.

~

THE NEW CAPTAIN, Beula Olin, chose the name THE GREEN NIGHT. It was assumed that it was a play on the Round Table and ERRANT names It was but only she knew the details. As a child of six, Beula was sold by her drug addicted parents to a pedophile ring for the dose of chemicals that took their pointless lives.

Her father had been an aggressive stock manipulator and her mother a political activist. Both of their successes brought them into the world of the elites and drugs. What neither realized was that they were both addictive personalities. They spiraled out of the upper circles into homeless dregs, valuing nothing beyond their next connection and fix.

Beula had been an unusually intelligent child. Thanks to her parents' genes and the selective and manipulative birthing program they subscribed to, she was only slightly below the math prodigy's IQ level. By the age of three, she could read and was solving quantum equations by the time she was five.

As her parents sank in life, she isolated herself as much as she could from them and lost herself in her world of chivalry and magic. She devoured fairy tales and epic books of fantasy. She immersed herself in the legends and myths of the dark and middle ages. Of all her books, stories about the Green Knight were her favorites. His role in literature of the myths includes his being a judge and tester of other knights.

After six years of abuse at the hands of the pedophile ring, Beula was scheduled to be a blood sacrifice at one of the cult's rituals. She was chained to an altar already stained with the blood of other children slaughtered in the years before. But before she could be murdered, she was bought by an elderly cult member who wanted her for himself.

It wasn't all altruistic. The man, whose last name was Olin, had lost his only child in a nasty divorce and was banned from ever contacting her through the bribed judge's order. For some reason, Beula reminded him of his daughter.

He had bought time with Beula the first time he'd seen her. He had no twisted motive — he only wanted to talk to the girl. He quickly realized how exceptional she was. He made his plans to purchase her while the gang was making preparations for the child's death.

When Olin made his offer, the cult was unsure. But he kept upping his offer until they could no longer say no. He was her Green Knight.

Olin never returned to the cult and never mistreated Beula. He adopted her and moved them to another planet. The child grew and came to her full potential in the Joint Military Academy. The man she came to call father was killed in an attack at the beginning of the Corporate War. Although he left her a sizable fortune, she had found her life in the military.

During the war, she served with Ash Kennett and was sent back to civilian life when the militaries downsized after the peace accord. But her love for the myths and legends of the literature was still a flame inside her imagination. When she saw the crew call from Round Table Ventures and a ship called THE ERRANT, she had to apply.

When she was given the refitted and re-engineered Taxexa Corporation cruiser, she knew what name to use — but instead of "Knight," she used "night." When asked about it, she would say it was named after the Aurora Borealis she had seen on several planets. No one questioned her, but she knew she hoped to do good things with her ship and be an example to the others.

CHAPTER TWENTY-SIX

THE SONG OF INDIA, a medium-sized indy ore hauler, responded to a distress call from a floundering space yacht. When INDIA pulled up near the pleasure craft, four other ships appeared from behind a nearby moon. It was instantly clear this was a pirate trap. The freight captain sent out an SOS.

Armed and EVA suited pirates moved the yacht closer to THE SONG OF INDIA while the others in the band surrounded the ship. These smallest and most maneuverable of ships, the yacht, were armed with pulse and laser weapons, each of which had been jerry-rigged to the decks. The freighter kept its airlocks closed as long as it could and listened to the demands of the pirates who fired warning shots over and around her.

A dozen Scorpion fighters abruptly appeared out of seemingly empty space. They took up firing positions covering all the pirates. Starfighter pilot Lt. Audie Spinks, the flight leader, parked his threatening fighter, almost touching the pirate yacht's front port. Using the same radio frequency the pirates had used to contact THE SONG OF INDIA, Spinks convinced the pirate leader to surrender or be vaporized.

The action added to the Lieutenant's luster, call sign "Lancelot," who was not only a skilled pilot but also popular with the bunk bunnies aboard THE GREEN NIGHT. He did lance a lot.

Captain Beula Olin wanted any excuse to wipe out all the small belligerent ships. The Scorpions were both elusive and seemed immune to the point defense weapons of the pirate ships. The tiny but deadly craft had shields unknown for such small-sized vessels. Their weapons inflicted exact and consequential damage on the large ship. All were dead in space within three minutes of the appearance of the first Scorpion.

Then THE GREEN NIGHT uncloaked and

revealed her weapons. The fight went out of the pirates instantly.

The crews were all brought aboard an empty cargo bay of THE GREEN NIGHT.

Where possible, Captain Olin assigned prize crews to the pirate ships. For the others, she used her tractor beam to tow them to a harbor.

Incidents like the one with THE SONG OF INDIA had become a significant loss to the pirate king.

The Round Table ships began to make a habit of answering calls from corporate traders because THE ERRANT and THE GREEN NIGHT were faster to respond than the sluggish and bureaucratic corp military. It didn't take long for the corporations to get the message.

The United Corporations were deadlocked on continuing the bribe payment to Bartholomew Lutz when they were still dealing with other pirates. The problem was all pirates were not affiliated with the Pirate King and tribute payment to Lutz had no impact on the autonomous pirates.

The United Corporation's conflict was the tribute the corporations paid while remaining vulnerable to other pirate factions versus the outstanding work Round Table Ventures did. However, they did agree to pay the submitted bills from Round Table Ventures.

The acquired yacht the pirates had used when trying to waylay THE JACK AND JILL was given as a prize to Santana Vanderhoff to refit and enjoy at his pleasure.

Within the next year, those plying the skull and crossbones trade in the systems were standing trial and facing execution. The once mysterious buccaneer hunter-killers weren't out of business, but a notable dent had been given them in their business.

WHEN CAPTAIN BEULA OLIN returned with her prizes, she was summoned to THE ERRANT's conference room. Commander Bywater was already there and congratulated Olin on her successful mission. When she was seated, there was a beep at the door.

"Come," Ash said.

Chief Engineer Starla Vanderhoff joined them.

"Chief," Ash motioned to a chair. To the newly promoted Captain he said, "It is important that we keep each other linked in on everything."

"Of course, Captain — or are you going to be our commodore?"

"As long as we're on the same screen, I don't see the need — nor do I have the desire. Neither do I think you'll need the interference, Captain."

"Thank you, Sir," Olin said.

"What I do expect are some innovations in tactics and even command structure. I'd like to keep learning together. Example — Lt. Commander Vanderhoff has made a discovery we will be instituting on THE ERRANT — and, I believe, you will probably want to the same on THE GREEN NIGHT."

"And," THE ERRANT's chief engineer said, "if I can add, to all new ships we add to the fleet."

"You've anticipated that, have you?" Ash asked with a slight grin.

"It seems only logical, Sir. I am sure we will acquire other ships as we go. Some of them are likely to be worthy additions, after father's refittings, to a fleet. A fleet can certainly expand our reach and service."

"With the people I've selected," Captain Olin said, "I am expecting great things, too, Captain."

"To understand this, you will need to close your eyes," Ash said to Beula. She did so. A glance and nod to Vanderhoff was the signal for her to begin.

"Captain Olin, can you still hear me?" Starla said from her nerolink.

"Of course."

"And me," Doc said, using the same system.

"Yes."

"And me," Ash joined in.

"Ten by 10," Beula Olin said.

"Open your eyes, Commander" Ash ordered.

She did.

"Notice none of us are actually speaking orally."

"Mary had a little lamb," Doc said, *"which very much surprised her parents."*

"We are using your nerolink," Lt. Commander Vanderhoff said.

Beula's eyes opened and flew back and forth in their sockets.

"The Captain's Ready Room is set up as a nero net. Anyone in this space can communicate with anyone else by merely thinking of them and speaking. It's something I've been working on with the Captain's permission and with some input from Commander Bywater."

"Can you hear me?" Beula said in her head.

"Yes," all three answered.

"Originally I came up with a system which went

through not only our individual chips but also involved our AIs. But Commander Bywater has convinced me that this could be too intrusive. Now the system works without AI automatic involvement — but it could be added if the individuals gave permission."

Out loud Ash said, "I want to set up nets for each department and link individuals together by their own permission and that of their section head."

"And we want to incorporate our own standardized encryption on both ends of each conversation," Doc said.

"I see the possibilities," Captain Olin said.

"Doc is working on rules, regs, and best practices. You'll see a copy of what we have so far in your inbox. We will be implementing it aboard THE ERRANT this week once we are out in the dark, away from everyone and everything."

"What is the range?" Olin wanted to know.

"A couple of kilometers is as far as we've tested it ," Vanderhoff said. "It's still 10 by 10 at that range. It's one of the things we need to keep testing. We do know it works in and around the ship — but how far beyond that we don't know, yet."

"The Scorpions will still have our radio links,"

Ash said, "but in the event one goes out, they could use this method. When you implement it on THE GREEN NIGHT, we'd like to know anything new, if anything, you learn about the system."

≈

COMMANDER LASHAWN BLUNIE, Ash's former tactical chief of THE ERRANT, took over the other captured cruiser. Blunie renamed it THE THRESHER. His great-great-great-great grandfather had served on a submarine by the same name that was lost in a deep ocean mission. Keeping the ship's name alive was Captain Blunie's way of honoring his forebearer.

The three ships worked independently and were able to cover the transport routes of the Matheus quadrant. It became clear that the indy ships had better protection than those corporations. This had to change.

CHAPTER TWENTY-SEVEN

The brutal pirate king still held dominion over the Matheus quadrant of the Kermerus galaxy — but his power was beginning to be questioned. Corporations and governments paid their required tributes while their ships kept to known space and still feared Lutz. The few who crossed outside now patrolled routes by accident or in desperate circumstances, invariably ran into pirate trouble. Some of the newer ships could outrun the pirates while others still fell prey to them. And occasionally a pirate vessel was lost during an engagement. This, however, was rare.

No one lived or worked in his end of the galaxy without paying tribute from money to crops, to ore, and yearly quotas from the corporations. Lutz practiced human slavery and ruled with savage cruelty. Captured sex slaves from children to middle age were loaded like cattle onto Lutz's ships, never to be seen or heard of again. The same was true of labor slaves of any age.

The Lutz legend grew in spite of Round Table Venture's incursions and rescues. Still, the news of each pirate ship lost did more than infuriate Bartholomew Lutz, it rattled him.

"How in hell do these assholes know where we will strike?" he asked Arluna Ito, his second in command, the only pirate he trusted. Even her striking cleavage and caramel colored skin warranted no attention from Lutz at the moment. He paced in his private castle bar. "Do they know where Deadwood is? Do we have a spy?"

"If we had a spy, how would they communicate with anyone in the galaxy?" Arluna answered the pirate master. She spread out on the couch, displaying one shapely leg along the leather while keeping her other foot on the carpet.

"I could take THE UNHOLY REVENGE out and try to find out. Take the fight to them."

"Oh, no," Lutz said. "If it comes down to a fight, I want your ship and THE BLACK DEATH to be together. They couldn't beat us together. But I don't want it to come to that."

"You've done all you can, haven't you? You got satellites out and you've built those two armed emplacements — one on each end of town."

"I can't just sit here and wait for them to find us."

"Then we have to go hunt them."

"How? Where?"

Arluna took a slug of her drink before she said, "Remember the raid we pulled on those three ships off of Ranvone?"

Lutz clawed back in his memory. "That little nothing planet with the six moons?"

"Yes. It was our first huge strike."

"We had ships behind each moon and we all sailed in at once."

"Blocking any escape route. We only had to blow up the lead ship before the other two gave up."

"Yeah, I remember."

"You picked up the little blond you kept so long. What was her name?"

"Cena something. I never cared about last names."

"You got her pregnant three times, didn't you?"

"And I got tired of getting rid of her little bastards before they were born."

"Well, as I remember, The Sugar Shack was glad to have her when you were through with her."

Lutz laughed. "She was one hot little piece."

"I never told you this, Bartholomew, but I was jealous."

"No. You?"

"Yes, me."

"Arluna, you are still the best I've ever had. I'd take you right now — if it weren't for Ash Kennett." He finished his drink in a single swallow and refilled his glass.

"My point was," Arluna said, "we could pull that Ranvone thing again. If we're lucky, we could get Ash Kennett and his pals all at once. We have nine frigates, five corvettes and two terrors — yours and mine."

"But how do we lure them there?"

"You still have your corporate contacts — use them to send a very valuable shipment of something — something that would draw all the king's men to protect it."

"They're not guarding corporate shippers — well, except for every once in a while."

"Then we can't count on that. But suppose one

of your corporate contacts could arrange for some valuable shipment through an independent cargo hauler. Wouldn't that be the kind of target the Kennett would protect?

"I think you've got something there, Arluna."

"I've got something everywhere," she said with a not so subtle grin pulling her shoulders back and thrusting the endowments forward.

"You always have," Lutz laughed. "But I want to make sure we're ready to wipe them out. Let's have every ship, every gun, rocket, and torpedoes cleaned and ready for a fight. While we do, I'll make the arrangements on the corporate end and put some bait out there."

"To do it right, we're talking about a month and a half at least."

"Then let's get started on it."

"I'll set the crew to work," Arluna said, getting to her feet.

"Suddenly I'm ready for a woman."

"Want me to send you one?"

"No, I want you, Arluna. Get the crews to work — and don't forget about the ground de-fense — then come back here. I want to test your everything."

～

THE MESSAGE AWAITING Jaxlynn and two of the others on the hidden comm site read, "Something big is up! Bigger than anything I've ever seen. Does Ranvone mean anything to you?" The message was from Sigma, the random Greek alphabet name she had assigned each of the four. To her, the S stood for "slave" as in "slave market."

Jaxlynn picked up on the sea change in the atmosphere around Bartholomew Lutz. Suddenly his libido was on fire. Since Jaxlynn was now responsible for the rotation and assignment of the harem members, she saw that satisfying his lust required two or three women at a time. Beyond that, she got no information from the women following their wild nights with the pirate leader.

"It was a sneak attack," the farmer, Delta for dirt, "wrote when he came online. It was years ago. That's where I was captured."

"I've heard the word before and felt it was always said with sadness," wrote Rho warehouse contact. To Jaxlynn, the Rho meant Rows of things.

"The pirates who were there still brag about it," wrote Sigma the slave market member of the group. "I've seen some excitement and anticipation all around the market. We're to expect a big influx when whatever happens is over."

"They have cleaned the planet side gun and rocket positions," wrote Rho. "I've heard they are doing the same on all the ships in dock in the space station."

"They have put defensive emplacements even out in the countryside," typed Delta. We are packing fruits and vegetables for ship use. They are slaughtering livestock and preparing them in the kind of containers that they use on ships."

"Then this something big will be our chance," Jaxlynn wrote. Her name was Pi, as in a piece of pie — although pie wasn't what she meant or felt like. "Are we going to be ready? We will get only one chance at this."

"Yes," Delta said.

"Yes," Rho agreed.

"Yes," typed Sigma.

No details were discussed, but each member of the team knew there were men and women, even teens, who had secreted away weapons and stolen armaments. This was for the day of uprising all the slaves on Deadwood had longed for and prayed for over the years.

"Let's check back here twice a day," Jaxlynn suggested as Pi. "We have to know quickly when it's time to begin."

They all agreed and said they were going to be

hyper vigilant for any signs, hints, and casual re-marks that would give them any more in-formation.

Jaxlynn knew it was time to send out a message.

CHAPTER TWENTY-EIGHT

At the end of three-and-a-half years, THE ERRANT, THE GREEN NIGHT, and THE THRESHER impacted the trade lanes on the Matheus quadrant. But there were such vast distances to cover. The improved FTL engines helped the Round Table's ships get to trouble spots as fast as possible. But the pirate threat was a long way from being contained. Besides saving the indy ships who were their clients, the main problem was how to find the pirate's lair.

Intelligence Lt. Commander Ethan Needham stitched together all the information the independent shippers had and built a picture. Needham would have made an ideal spy. He was average height and weight with no distinguishing features. His hair was light brown, his eyes hazel, and his facial features were neither remarkable nor memorable. But his mind was quick and made leaps not evident to others.

In a meeting he requested with Captain Kennett, the Lt. Commander said, "Sir, I have a growing notion that the pirates might well be on a forgotten planet on the outer edge of the galaxy. None of the data we've collected spells that out — however, it does point in that direction."

"Where exactly are you talking about?"

"May I, Sir," Needham said as he stepped over to the Captain's computer. Ash sat back out of the way as the Lt. Commander pulled up the holographic map of the Matheus quadrant of the galaxy on the Captan's desk. The young man crossed back around until he stood across from Ash.

"Before the war, Sir, Lancet Corporation thought they had discovered a silver plante right here." Needham enlarged the space around the dot which grew until it became dominant and the name "Deadwood" appeared near it with coordinates.

"They invested heavily, including a city they called Butte before they concluded that the silver wasn't as plentiful as they believed. The corporation had built a space station in geosynchronous orbit. But they lost their EVA suits on this venture and ended up abandoning it and declaring bankruptcy. Even after the war no one has been interested in the place because it so far out and it has so little to offer."

"So this — Deadwood — is an abandoned planet with some infrastructure? Sound ideal for a pirate home base."

"That was my thinking, Sir, and why I wanted to bring it to your attention."

"Excellent work, Lt. Commander. Can you keep digging into this?"

"Absolutely, Sir. And one more thing, Captain."

"Yes?"

"We've been inflicting some rather substantial damage to their operation — and we've cost them several ships."

"Agreed."

"Well, Sir, if it were me — I'd be trying to figure out a way to get back at whoever has been attacking me and costing me so much."

"Have you seen anything like that?"

"No, Sir, but I think all of our ships should be

on the lookout for anything suspicious — abnormal."

"Everything we do and see is somewhat abnormal, Commander. Do you have anything more specific?"

Lt. Commander Needham shook his head and shrugged his shoulders. "But I believe if all the Captains and G2 sections are aware, they might recognize something when it happens."

"Good thought. I'll pass the word along. Thank you, Lt. Commander Needham. I am impressed."

"Thank you, Sir. Nothing more than my job, Sir."

"It's a great deal more — and we both know it. Keep it up. Dismissed."

ASH WAS in his Ready Room when there was a chime announcing that someone was outside his door. Glancing at his door monitor he saw his NCOIC, the Briquet.

"Come," Ash said, and the door opened.

She stepped up to Ash's desk and snapped a salute. Ash returned the salute and offered her a chair.

"What can I do for you, Senior Master Chief?"

"I'd like to be reassigned, Sir."

"I beg your pardon?"

"Reassigned, Sir. I'll be glad to accept a demotion if that's what it takes."

"You don't like THE ERRANT?"

"No, Sir. It's not the ship — or you, or anyone else on board. I'm not a paper pusher. I need to be back with the marines. I'm a fighter, Captain. I have really tried to be a good NCOIC ...."

"And you've been an excellent one."

"Thank you, Sir, but — this isn't what I signed on for. I want to be back where the troops are taking on the pirates one on one."

Ash leaned back, steepling his fingers below his chin.

"I see. Well, Senior Master Chief, I won't demote you. You have earned your rank and your title. What do you suggest?"

"How about a primary boarding party — a force recon type team — the first in and the last out — any time — anywhere? A dirty jobs team."

"I can see the value of that. But who would you suggest as NCOIC, Master Chief Dardean?"

"No, Sir. That would kill him. I'd actually like for him to be my second in command. He's done the cargo thing about as long as he can stand it."

"You two have talked it over, I presume."

"Pillow talk — and more, if you know what I mean, Sir."

"That's already more than I'd need to know," Ash said before hurrying on. "Then whom do you suggest? NCO's at your level don't do a thing without a damn good plan. You're suggesting this because you know someone who you think will be better at the job than you are. Who is it?"

"Master Chief Deron Ficken. He's NCOIC of G8."

"Finance."

"Very organized, a master of paperwork — respected by everyone who knows him or has ever worked with him. Honest — fair," Birgitta Perry paused before she said, "His file is in your in box, Sir."

Ash checked his screen and saw the folder. He clicked it and opened the file. Reading over it, he saw Ficken unconsciously nodded his head.

"I see he's eligible for a bump to Senior Master Chief."

"The ship's NCOIC slot requires that doesn't it, Sir?"

"You knew that before you came in here, didn't you?"

Perry didn't blush as she said, "Seeing a

problem without having a solution is whining. Marines don't whine, Sir." Her nut-brown eyes held steady.

"Let me closely examine his file and I'll get back to you."

"Thank you, Sir." She snapped another salute.

"At ease, Senior Chief," Ash said. She lowered her salute as he said, "This dirty jobs team you came up with — it's something every ship should have, don't you think?"

"I do, Sir. If we get one up and functioning, we could train up others."

"Is your duffle already packed, Senior Chief?"

"No, Sir. Without your approval this is all talk."

"I think if I don't approve this, Senior Chief, you'll want to kick my ass."

It took a considerable effort on the Briquet's part not to smile — but she kept her composure with a swallow.

"Go finish packing your things and have Master Chief Ficken report to me in an hour. I'm sure this is all a formality, but with your recommendation and your team idea, I'm certain this is a good plan."

CHAPTER TWENTY-NINE

Ash declared two weeks of R&R for their crews at Xanadu Transit. THE GREEN NIGHT and THE THRESHER were still out on patrol. The station was in a rapid building phase with new hotels, bars, shops, a terraforming museum, and a merchant spacer's academy planning to take over one complete level. Space tourism cruises were putting the station on their routes. Permanent residents had high rise penthouses or patio homes and a golf course.

It surprised Doc to get an invitation to lunch at one of the palatial restaurants from Starla Vanderhoff. Doc was back in his hooded robe and the young Lt. Commander wore a short skirt which showed off her long shapely legs and sparkling multi patterned blouse.

They ordered, ate and enjoyed an excellent Grand Marnier after-meal drink.

"You still haven't told me what this is all about," Doc said, swirling his liqueur in his stemmed glass. "I'm presuming this is not official."

"No. It's personal. I'd like for you to put on your clerical collar or counselor's hood."

"OK. I'm at your confidential service, my lady."

"Doc, you know how satisfying I find life on THE ERRANT."

"It shows in your creativity — but also in the attitude of those in your department. You are respected professionally and admired personally."

"That's wonderful to know. And to hear it said. I don't think father had any idea when he suggested I sign on — but, Doc, these are my kind of people — only I never knew they existed before."

"So what's the problem? I'm sure there's a problem in here somewhere?'

Starla took a full drink of her Grand Marnier and set the glass back on the table before she said, "I must have father issues — although I don't know what they are. I love my dad and always have. He's the smartest man in the world, I think. He claims I put him to shame with my insights and creativity — but I've been through the university intensely where he only hit the high points between parties — at least as he tells it."

"No, that's true. Your old man was a party beast in his day. Your mother was the only one who could tame him — and even she couldn't for long."

"Oh, I know all about their divorce. Before she died, Mother told me that her time with Father was the best days of her life — especially when I was born and they were learning to be a family. She said she should have been more forgiving — that despite everything, he was the love of her life."

"You know Santana has resigned himself to having lost you to THE ERRANT — and I'm not sure he's truly sorry. He sees how happy you are. He glows at the very mention of your name."

They sat in silence for several moments before Doc broke it by saying, "I don't think your father is your problem."

"No," she admitted with a sigh. "It's Captain Kennett."

Doc's eyes darted from side to side, and he shook his head slowly.

"I'm still missing something here."

Starla licked her lips and grabbed a breath. "I think I'm in love with Ash Kennett."

This idea pushed Doc back into his chair.

"I know he knows I exist — as a member of his crew — as his Chief Engineer — but —." She stopped because she couldn't put words together to explain herself. "He's never done or said anything which would lead me to think — that he thinks — and I haven't said or done anything out of line either." She studied Doc as the silence continued. "I'm not as young as I look. I'm 35. I'm not a child — and I know I've had a sheltered life in many ways. But Doc, I've never felt the way I do about the Captain for another living person."

Doc held up his hand to stop her.

"Starla, the ways of the heart are as much a mystery to me as to any other man — or woman. Ash had a catastrophe in his life several years back. That's why he was a miner — a sole miner on an asteroid with only his implant for company for a couple of years."

"Zullie."

"Right. She's sarcastic — and can be hilarious, he says — and that's what kept him going. I don't know if he's recovered — or if he ever will. I can't explain the situation, but suffice it to say it was a matter of broken trust. Will he ever love someone again? I don't know. I doubt he's even thought about it. He doesn't want to let his mind even go there."

"Knowing that helps me, Doc. Thank you. And I understand you're not breaking any confidences for the Captain. I also fully understand the problems of on board romance. I don't want to create or take part in that kind of trouble. But I had to talk to someone other than Phaedra. She tried to help — but this is way out of her scope."

"Have you considered the possibility that this is merely a passing thing — a phase — a fascination — something that won't last?"

"Oh, yes," she said, "for most of our first year. And I even hoped that was what it was. After two and half years, I don't believe that any more. And I get it that this is only my problem. The Captain may not — most likely does not — feel the same way — even a little. And he is the Captain."

"The loneliest position on the ship. It's the stuff of tragedy, for sure."

"I know. And that's what I'm living with — but I needed to share, Doc. I hope this doesn't put a burden on you — or with your relationship with the Captain."

"I'll be all right, Starla. I hope you will be, too. Maybe a magic door will open and things will change."

"We both know there's little chance of that. Just having put it into words has helped, Doc. I pledge to you, I won't do anything inappropriate."

"I never thought you would." Doc took his last swallow of his drink before he said, "Please talk to me anytime you need to, Starla."

"Thank you, Doc. I most likely won't — but it's good to know you have offered."

CHAPTER THIRTY

THE ERRANT joined THE THRESHER back on patrol. THE GREEN NIGHT returned to Xanadu Transit for two weeks of leave. THE THRESHER would rotate in for R&R when THE GREEN NIGHT was back on patrol.

The independent shippers and cruise operators had nothing but praise for the Round Table's actions and presence. Isolated attacks on the smallest shippers continued to occur, and it caused even more of the little fish to gather under the Round Table umbrella.

Ash and Doc had expanded their intelligence networks through their clients. Tiny pieces of information were gleaned and the picture of the overall pirate operation became clearer.

Intelligence Lt. Commander Ethan Needham sought out Ash one day during lunch.

"More news?" Ash asked, looking up at the nondescript officer.

"More like a new mystery, Sir. I apologize for interrupting your meal."

"Not a problem," Ash said, standing and taking his tray to the dirty dish conveyer belt. As he and Lt. Commander Needham walked toward CIC, Ash asked, "What do you have?"

"Only a couple of words — but it's about how we came across them. I want you to see this, Sir."

"Lead on," Ash said, gesturing Needham to move ahead.

Inside CIC, Needham showed Ash the display on a screen from an oscilloscope. The squiggly green lines up and down the screen exhibited the electronic elements of a radio signal.

"We have been receiving these pulses from some very widely dispersed satellites. At first glance they seem to be standard scanning signals."

"Somebody is probing and screening for movement along certain paths?"

"Primarily along shipping lanes. They reflect

nothing from us because we're so stealthy. We either reflect the signals so they don't bounce back or we just absorb them. And without a return signal, we can't be seen."

"I understand. Isn't this the kind of scans we and every other ship uses?"

"Yes, Sir. All ports, inhabited planets, and even astroids do the same."

"All right — so? Why is this significant?"

"Look at this." Lt. Commander Needham said, switching the screen's output to show two signals side by side.

"Two signals. OK."

"But different."

Ash examined the dual display.

"They look identical to me."

"They are, Sir, except for this." The intelligence officer pointed to a tiny pulse which was on the edge of one signal. He enlarged the signal and the tiny variant was expanded.

"What is that?"

"That insignificant blip, Sir, is an encoded two-word message we kept missing until I zoomed in on the signal. That's when I saw there was something there."

"What are the words?"

"Ranvone ambush."

"What does that mean?"

"Ranvone is a dead planet with a half dozen moons."

"Is it important for some reason?"

"Not that I can find. There are no records of anything happening in the past hundred — or even further back, as far as I can find. If the site is important for some reason, it wasn't ever recorded."

"What does the 'ambush' part of it mean?"

"I don't know that either, Sir. That's why it's a mystery."

Ash examined the signal and repeated the words, "Ranvone ambush." After a moment he ask Needham, "A warning or a call to arms?"

The intelligence officer shrugged his shoulders and shook his head. "One thing I am sure of is that it wasn't meant to draw attention to itself."

"Then it wasn't intended for the people who sent the message."

"It wasn't meant for them to notice it, I'd say, Sir. But we surely have."

~

MASTER CHIEF DERON FICKEN was promoted to Senior Master Chief in a ceremony held on an empty cargo deck. Ficken was 40 something, a spare but not skinny black man with a broad forehead and croaky voice. The new SMC was then installed as THE ERRANT's NCOIC.

For Ash, there was only a single major difference he could detect between his previous NCOIC and the new one. Ficken set a faster pace in executing the reports the ship required. Even as pirate hunters, a ship as massive as THE ERRANT required a significant amount of daily, weekly and monthly forms and documents. Even though most of this was done electronically, the information needed by command and by the lower ranks had to be generated, distributed, and acknowledged.

The Dirty Jobs team SMC Perry organized were all hard charging men and women who took pride in their individual skills. The Briquet had told those who wanted to apply that they were there to be the jagged, scalpel-sharp, point of the spear. "If anyone is to get killed when we're on a boarding or ground operation," she warned them, "I want it to be one of us. So we had better be prepared for anything."

She trained them hard, and they loved it. The adrenalin rush of combat was what these people lived for. They learned to communicate exclusively over the nerolinks and developed their own codes to shortcut orders, warnings, and messages.

"If you want a promotion in this outfit, you're going to have to out fight, out shoot, or out run Master Chief Dardean." Her scarfaced second became the image many on the team aspired to. Any wounds they would get, they pledged to each other to have repaired but to leave the external marks. Scars were a badge of honor to this team.

When the team got to the point SMC Perry wanted, two Master Chiefs were farmed out to THE GREEN NIGHT and THE THRESHER to develop Dirty Jobs teams for each vessel.

***

A brief battle between THE THRESHER and a pirate ship called SIN added a second cruiser to the Round Table Fleet. The battered vessel, SIN, was sent back to Xanadu Transit for the attention of Santana Vanderhoff. This ship, like the others captured, was a stolen mothballed corporation war craft.

Ash called a meeting of ships' captains aboard THE ERRANT.

"Recommendations for someone to assume

command of our latest addition?" Ash asked when Captains Olin and Lashawn Blunie were seated in the conference room.

"Don't you already have someone in mind?" Captain Blunie asked.

"I could fill the slot, but I wanted to be fair to you two as well. You've worked with officers who might be ready to assume command — so I'm asking."

Captains Olin and Blunie exchanged looks and then Captain Olin said, "I believe my XO deserves her own command."

"Commander Rondalyn Archard," Ash said, remembering the 30-year-old looking voluptuous black officer with a shaved head.

"I agree," said the jowly faced, mahogany skinned Captain Blunie. He had deep-set eyes which were intense. "I worked with her in the war and on THE ERRANT. She'd make an excellent captain."

"Then I concur," Ash said. "Captain Olin, do you want to approach her with the offer of promotion and command?"

"I believe it would be better coming from you, Ash," Olin said, intending to move from their titled addressing of each other to a more casual approach.

"Why?" he asked.

Just then there was a chime and Ash looked toward the door expecting a steward with coffee. "Come," he said.

The door opened and Commander Bywater stood there. He stepped in.

"Doc?" Ash asked.

"Come in, Doc," said Beula Olin.

Doc was wearing his kitchen chef whites and appeared confused.

Ash wrinkled his forehead as Doc joined the trio at the conference table.

"I'm here." Doc said.

"What's up," Ash asked, looking at the other officers across the table.

"I invited him," Beula said. "Doc, have you had time to do as I requested?"

"I have," he said. "He agreed and so do I."

"What?" Ash asked.

"Captain Blunie and I have a proposal. Doc has joined us as an owner of Round Table Ventures. Evidently Yardmaster Vanderhoff agrees with it."

"Then it's time I was let in on this, don't you think?" Ash said a little frustrated.

"We want you to move up to Rear Admiral," Beula said. "We know you don't want the rank nor the responsibility," she went on quickly. "But the reality of our company is that as both a partner and as the first captain, you are our leader. With the addition of another ship and a new captain in our ranks, it's time for someone to take the reins — especially if and when — because we all know it's going to happen — we come together in a fight."

"We'd need a command authority," Lashawn Blunie said, "and to all of us that's you, like it or not, Ash."

Ash sat back in his chair and rubbed his chin.

"Two stars on your collar and let your XO take over as Captain of THE ERRANT. It's not that hard," Beula said.

Ash looked at Doc. "You and Santana agree on this?"

"Obviously," Doc said with a smile. "That's why I'm here."

"You don't even have to change your quarters," Beula said. "If you want to enlarge the XO's quarters, I'm sure Yardmaster Vanderhoff could make that happen."

The conference room was silent for a full minute until Ash finally sighed. He didn't want to say, "yes" but it seemed to be out of his hands.

"All right," Ash finally said biting his tongue.

As the meeting broke up, Ash asked Doc to remain behind.

"I think you were right?"

"About your being an Admiral?"

"No. About my needing a family. Doc, this isolates me even more. I had forgotten that what I hated about command is the loneliness. I've just accepted more of that."

"Did you? You're an Admiral now, Ash. Figure out how to fix that."

CHAPTER THIRTY-ONE

A joint promotion ceremony was held with Doc, as one of the owners of Round Table Ventures, presiding. Ash was presented with two solid four-pointed stars and became the first Admiral of the company. Travis Phan, Ash's XO, was promoted to the Captain of THE ERRANT. Commander Rondalyn Archard was promoted to Captain of the yet to be renamed captured pirate ship, SIN.

Phan appeared to be in his late 30s, almost as tall as Ash, athletic with a prominent Adam's apple and thin mustache. His choice for XO was Lt. Commander Greta Camus, a blond who wore her platinum hair in a bun. The oval faced Camus had light scintillating blue eyes and a no-nonsense demeanor. She stepped up to full Commander and assumed the position.

Ash didn't want a full G level command staff, but he did claim Lt. Commander Ethan Needham as his G-1 Intelligence. The very average looking officer was promoted to full Commander and became part of Ash's minimal staff. NCOIC Deron Ficken had a recommendation for the Admiral's chief NCO.

Officer's country was reconfigured, so that there was a space directly above THE ERRANT's CIC for the Admiral's Fleet Command Information Center and a Ready Room for the Admiral. In the new CIC Ash had a command chair looking down on the 3D hologram of whatever battle space had been dialed up.

～

"ADMIRAL," Commander Needham reported to Ash in his ready room, "This maybe nothing but it sounds suspicious to me, Sir."

"What is it, Commander?" Ash asked from his desk.

"Two cargo ships under our protection, THE

KEY WEST and THE CATALINA have been asked to take a full load each of disco-lite to the space port Sultana."

"What's odd about that? Ports need disc-o-lite to refuel ships, don't they?"

"Yes, Sir, but not this much at one time. And The Octavio Corporation is an energy company. It has plenty of its own vessels to transport such a valuable cargo. And there are a couple of more things rather curious about it?"

"Go on," Ash said, sitting back and giving Needham his full attention.

"Shipments like these normally go from the home corporation to their ports on company ships. THE KEY WEST and THE CATALINA are independents. They very rarely get assignments from a corporation and certainly not one this lucrative."

"I see what you mean."

"And the most suspicious fact is that the route the ships were to take were specified by Octavio Corporation. And it runs right through the Ranvone system and all of its moons."

"Have these two ships shoved off yet?"

"No, Sir. But they are scheduled to leave at 0500 local time tomorrow."

"How long will it take them to get to Ranvone system?"

"These are slow freighters, Sir. About two months."

"I'll see if we can't get our new ship ready in time to join us there."

CHAPTER THIRTY-TWO

It took only a month for captured ship SIN to be refitted and rechristened as THE ALASKA. The new commanding officer, Captain Rondalyn Archard, never gave a reason for her choice of names. Santana Vanderhoff shifted work dockets to an all-hands-on-deck mode for THE ALASKA.

The cruiser was patched, the ship's exterior was reworked for armor and stealth, plus THE ALASKA was rearmed in record time. It had a two week shake down cruise and its few problems were quickly addressed when it returned to Xanadu Transit. Then it was off to join the Round Table fleet.

~

ASH'S PLAN was to have THE GREEN NIGHT and THE ALASKA shadow the two cargo ships. THE ALASKA would do so cloaked while THE GREEN NIGHT was clearly escorting the pair of indy haulers.

Ash stationed the cloaked ERRANT and THRESHER above and below the planet Ranvone. The distances here were measured in astronomical units, approximately 150 million kilometers. The Ranvone system was about 50 AU wide, or 7.5 billion kilometers. On command, both ships could FTL into any plotted position in the system within one second.

Both vessels put out baseball sized passive sensors to orbit the planet and each of its moons. On each orbit the sensors had line-of-sight shots at either THE ERRANT or THE THRESHER. The probes communicated with the ship, which launched it by micro burst laser. In the dark emptiness of space, no trace of laser shots showed, and thus the communication was direct, invisible, and private. The Round Table ships monitored their orbiting instruments and sat back to wait. It would be a week and a half before THE KEY WEST and

THE CATALINA would pass through the Ranvone system.

~

THE PIRATE SHIPS of Bartholomew Lutz arrived in the Ranvone system three days before the cargo vessels were scheduled to pass through it. Five corvettes and nine frigates took up stations behind the different moons hidden from the expected paths of the incoming freighters. None of these vessels appeared to have means of cloaking, which was not available through any corporation during the corporate wars. Finally two terrors, T-Rex full battleships arrived. One waited beside the planet Ranvone while the other stayed alone behind the farthest moon.

Admiral Kennett as well as Captains Travis Phan and Lashawn Blunie tagged each of the pirate ships and assigned a red tag to each. Since none of the outlaw vessels had a responder or name, the Round Table cruisers ascribed a number designator for their purposes.

When the two cargo ships, THE KEY WEST and THE CATALINA, along with THE GREEN NIGHT and the cloaked ALASKA, approached the system, THE THRESHER updated all of them of the lurking pirates. All four battle cruisers called their crews to battle stations.

One of the T-Rex battleships shot forward as soon as the freighters were in the center of the Ranvone system. The pirate ship hailed the haulers and commanded that they stop. But even as the last word of the declaration was spoken, the massive ship fired on THE GREEN NIGHT. Captain Beula Olin returned fire instantly. Missiles, torpedoes, pulse, and laser weapons as well as the railgun shots were exchanged.

Two squadrons of Socrpions poured out of launch ports on both the starboard and port side of THE GREEN NIGHT. Flight leader, Lt. Audie Spinks, call sign "Lancelot," raced toward the T-Rex. The deadly dwarf starfighters swarmed like wasps weaving, jigging and jagging, darting and avoiding the bigger enemy ships attempt to target lock them.

The other hiding pirate corvettes and frigates moved in on THE GREEN NIGHT at flank speed. Each began firing on THE GREEN NIGHT as soon as they were able.

THE ALASKA uncloaked and turned its attention on the corvettes and frigates. At Ash's command, THE ERRANT and THE THRESHER jumped into the system and began unloading fire on all the pirate ships.

The pirate ships had difficulty acquiring target locks on any of the Round Table cruisers because of their stealth design and signal absorbing armor. The space was quickly teaming with Scorpions from all the other ships.

Lancelot released a limpet mine, a focused mini-EMP device alongside the T-Rex. As he darted away, he remotely turned on the magnetic locks which attached the weapon to the port side of the battleship. Another Scorpion did the same to the underside of the T-Rex. On a command from Lancelot, both devices were triggered and focused Electro Magnetic Pulses were sent through the T-Rex.

This left the enormous ship dead in space. All ithe electronics on the ship went dark. All its circuits fried. Not even their backup system could reboot it. Since this also killed the T-Rex's shields, all the munitions from the Round Table ships pulverized the ship, but once it was defenseless, they turned their attention to the incoming frigates and corvettes.

Two corvettes were torn apart by railgun fire from THE ERRANT and THE THRESHER. THE GREEN NIGHT and THE ALASKA ripped into the pirate's larger frigates. The outlaw ships were unable to successfully lock in on any Round Table vessel.

THE GREEN NIGHT, THE THRESHER, and THE ALASKA continued to take on the various remaining pirate ships. Deadly munitions of every kind laced across the Ranvone system and the pirates were clearly taking the brunt of the damage. Soon the corvettes and frigates were pounded into submission, even those who attempted to flee the battle space.

The second T-Rex, the one still hidden behind the planet Ranvone, broke its place as the pirate fleet was obviously getting the worst of the fight. This T-Rex raced away, leaping from behind one moon to another.

CHAPTER THIRTY-THREE

Ash ordered Captain Travis Phan to recall his starfighters. He told the rest of the fleet to continue the fight with the other pirates, but he was sending THE ERRANT after the escaping T-Rex. THE GREEN NIGHT, THE THRESHER and THE ALASKA were to finish the battle of Ranvone, kill any pirates who would not surrender and destroy all the pirate ships.

Ash's G-1 officer, Commander Ethan Needham, sent the coordinates of the planet Deadwood to Captain Travis Phan. Ash ordered Phan to take THE ERRANT out of the Ranvone system and make a cloaked run to the pirate home base. The Admiral also ordered Captain Phan to ready his Dirty Jobs team to be ready for an EVA assault.

An hour and a half later THE ERRANT dropped out of FTL in sight of the geosynchronous space port above the pirate city of Butt. Captain Phan maneuvered his ship near the upper level of the spinning platform.

Senior Master Chief Birgitta Genoveva Perry and her baker's dozen fully armored Dirty Jobs team shot out of THE ERRANT's starboard launch ramp. They pierced the ship's electronic cloak, using jets of nitrogen at their ankles to propel them. They landed on the space station gangway and ripped the airlock doors open as they charged in.

Perry and another DJ team member dropped pirates scrambling for oxygen masks in the hallways. MC Dixon Dardean split up the rest of the team and directed them to the station's power plant and docks.

Chief Perry and her companions reached the command-and-control hub and stormed in. The unsuspecting operators were drinking and drowsing. When the Briquet shoved her way in the pirates leapt to their feet and threw their hands into the air. She sent back the signal, "Alpha team — Europa! Repeat, Europa!"

"There's a T-Rex headed this way," SMC Perry said through the speakers at the side of her helmet as she held a blaster rifle at her waist aimed at the chief operator.

"Which one? THE BLACK DEATH or THE UNHOLY REVENGE?" asked the one seemingly in charge.

"Since they don't have ID tags or responders, it's hard to tell. Who are the Captains of each of them."

"Bartholomew Lutz is captain for THE BLACK DEATH. Arluna Ito is captain of THE UNHOLY REVENGE."

"I'll bet we're waiting for THE BLACK DEATH. For my credits, Lutz is a coward and ran when he saw the rest of his fleet getting their asses kicked. Whichever one shows up, you will report everything as nominal. If you use any code words or phrases, you die right where you sit. Do you understand?"

"Yes, ma'am," the shaken sloppy coverall wearing pirate said.

"Get back to your seat and check your scanner."

The thick but soft man sat back down and checked his equipment. "There's nothing out there," he said. "Where did you come from?"

The other pirate on duty, gaunt with a patchy attempt at growing a beard, remained standing with his hands still above his shoulders.

"If you screw with us, you'll think we came from hell."

Over her headset SMC Perry heard, "Gamma — Europa! Repeat, Europa!"

The Briquet knew the power plant was secure.

A few minutes later the report came in, "Beta and Delta — Europa! Repeat, Europa!" All the docking ports and the remaining pirate crew were under control.

The Dirty Jobs team was relieved, and they returned to THE ERRANT to recharge their jets. They then crammed themselves into the ship's shuttle and dropped into the atmosphere of the planet headed for the town of Butt.

"Captain Phan," Ash called the ship's Captain.

"Sir."

"Make note that we need two drop ships for each of our vessels."

"Right you are, Sir."

"I think we need to pull away from the station. There's no telling from which direction that T-Rex will approach. Put us in a position to be able to attack it no matter which port it might pick."

"Aye, aye, Sir."

~

THE ABSENCE of most pirates from the town was going to be the slaves only chance. Jaxlynn Shellanberger signaled her co-conspirators at their second of the day check-in time that now was the time for their uprising. It took a little over an hour for the captives to arm themselves. Six hours brought those from the farms, fields, and mines to town.

The first face-to-face meeting of Pi, Sigma, Rho, and Delta took place in the town square at a defaced monument to the defunct Lancet Corporation. Sigma, the manager of the slave market, was a full-figured woman with mostly gray hair. She had been a medical billing clerk in the IT department of her firm before her capture. Sigma's name was Marilinda.

Rho was a muscular-looking man in his thirties who stacked the rows of shelves of the pirate warehouse. He used a computer to keep track of the inventory. His name was Octavio.

Delta's name was Nguyen. He was a gaunt and ropy elderly man who ran the pirate farms using the computer operated irrigation, planting and harvesting equipment.

They were all surprised when they learned Pi

was such a young woman. She explained her advanced computer major and that her name was Jaxlynn. It was unquestioned that she was their leader.

Over the next few hours they rooted out the pirates left behind. Most were old, fat and drunks or addicts. All were herded into the flat space before the defaced corporate monument. Some had sobered up and realized what was happening. They were now the captives and faced a seething mob of slaves. They huddled in fear knowing only Bartholomew Lutz himself could save them.

~

THE DIRTY JOBS team had HALO jumped from the packed shuttle at twenty-two thousand meters (seventy-two thousand feet). They didn't trigger their ankle jets until one hundred fifty meters (five hundred feet).

They landed outside of town and split into two groups to approach the town center from each end of the main street. The former slaves had their lined captors up against a wall and had formed a firing squad.

A burst of the Briquet's blaster into the air halted the pending execution. The crowd turned to see seven fully armored marines. A burst from MCP Dardean at the opposite end of town caused the crowd to whirl and see a similar group there.

"Everyone put your guns on the ground!" SMC Perry said loudly through her helmet speakers. "We can kill you all before you can get off even a couple of rounds!"

The former slaves did as instructed, but many did so with tears streaming down their faces. Jaxlynn refused to put her weapon down.

The Dirty Jobs team moved in and had the crowds step back.

"Who are you and what do you want?" the young woman asked. "I'm ready to die here. I won't go back to the way things were."

While Jaxlynn held her position and her weapon, a rifle she'd taken off the body of a harem guard she had knifed in the back, the Briquet removed her helmet.

"I'm Senior Master Chief Birgitta Perry of the Round Table freighter, THE ERRANT. We are here to liberate everyone captured and enslaved by Bartholomew Lutz."

The crowd looked at each other.

"Please put your weapon down," SMC Perry said. "We mean you no harm."

Members of DJ Team began collecting weapons — even hoes and knives.

"Who is Round Table?" Jaxlynn asked.

"Friends," the Briquet said, lowering her rifle. "Friends who came to set you free. Pirates will never hurt you again."

Jaxlynn let the rifle slip to the ground and fell to her knees crying.

CHAPTER THIRTY-FOUR

THE BLACK DEATH arrived in system and hailed the space station.

The relief team stayed out of view of the comm camera but kept their weapons aimed at the head of the two pirates on duty. The sloppy coverall wearing pirate sat forward and reached for the connect button.

"Careful," the marine in body armor whispered. "Your life is on the line. Unless you're willing to die for Lutz, play it straight."

The pirate cleared his throat, pressed the button and said, "This is The Serpent's Nest, Captain. Go ahead."

"Anything happen since we left?"

"Not a thing. Were you expecting something?"

"No. I just wanted to be sure."

"Is the rest of the fleet behind you?"

"Just extend my docks and open the clamps!" Lutz said belligerently.

"Aye, aye, Captain."

The second pirate, the gaunt one with a patchy beard, pressed another button and three docks extended from the station. Each dock was covered by telescoping tramways.

THE BLACK DEATH eased up to its home port by computer controlled adjustments. When it was in place, the gaunt pirate in the control center secured the docking clamps.

The massive vessel powered down and captured pirates began to stream down the docks. The pirates were puzzled to find the airlock doors battened down from the inside of the station.

One pirate looked up to see a stream of Scorpion fighters pour out of a hole in space. His mouth was agape as his crew mates caught site of the starfighters. At that moment THE ERRANT uncloaked and began pouring munitions down on THE BLACK DEATH.

From the bridge of his shaking craft,

Bartholomew Lutz crawled back to his captain's chair and ordered his crew to power up.

Depleted 30 millimeter uranium shells ripped into and through THE BLACK DEATH. Carefully aimed slugs tore into the engine room and disabled the main reactor. By the time the pirates hurrying to disembark returned to their battle stations, most of their weapons had been disabled. Missiles and torpedos impacted the ship's hull from bow to stern.

Captain Phan didn't employ any EMPs because he wanted to capture the ship for Round Table Ventures. He did, however, continue to pound the craft until it was disabled as a fighting platform.

The air locks on the station opened and armored marines gushed out of every dock. The pirates threw up their hands and were ordered to their knees.

It required an hour for the marines to empty THE BLACK DEATH. When only Captain Bartholomew Lutz remained on board, Admiral Ash Kennett boarded the pirate space station and came down to THE BLACK DEATH's dock.

The marines had disarmed and secured every member of the crew when the Admiral stepped up to the ship in body armor, a blaster in his hand.

Ash made his way to the bridge accompanied by two marines. They found Lutz sitting in his captain's chair, his arms on the armrests. Ash released the catches on his helmet and removed it.

"I thought it would be you," Lutz said. "An admiral now. Well, well, haven't we come up in the world?"

"What a disgusting man you are," Ash said.

"You're just saying that because I killed your whore of a wife."

"No, I'm saying it because you wasted your life inflicting as much pain on others as you could. You could have used your abilities for so much more."

"What fun would that have been?" Lutz sneered a cruel smile. "While it lasted, I had all the power any man could have ever wanted. And I enjoyed it to the fullest. What more could any man ask for?"

"To be remembered for bringing peace and happiness to our world. And not going to hell to burn forever."

"Don't believe in hell." Lutz flipped open his arm rest and snatched a blaster pistol there.

Ash shot the pirate king in the chest. Lutz

froze and gasped one last breath as the blaster slipped from his hands.

The marines were bringing their weapons up as the events ended.

The Admiral stepped up to Lutz's crumpling body and said, "Glad I can help you find out. No need to let me know how hot it is."

Lutz knew that he was dying, but he never expected it to come with so much pain. He sagged in his chair.

"Remove his body," Ash ordered. "I want this ship rigged to take back to Xanadu." Then Ash paused and said, "Belay that order about the ship. Make sure it's secure here and set a guard.

THE POPULATION of Deadwood was delighted to meet Ash when he came dirtside. He stood in front of the old sculpture in the town square and addressed the people.

"Ours is not a passenger ship but everyone of you is welcome to return with us."

"How about those who were sold and taken away," Marilinda, the slave market manager, called out from the crowd. The gray-haired, full figured woman added, "We have meticulous records of each and where they were sent."

"Sounds like a mission we can undertake," Ash answered.

The crowd cheered.

"What's going to happen to Butt — and Dead-wood?" The question came from Nguyen the ropy elderly farmer.

"I am claiming this town, this city and the space station above for Round Table Ventures. That's our company. I think our first order of business will be to rename it all. Any suggestions?"

"This place has wonderful dirt for farming. If you want it to grow how about giving land away for the people who want new start. And call it Homestead."

"I like that," Ash smiled. "I'll ask my partners. Any suggestions for a town name?"

"Almanac?" again Nguyen suggested. "It's still the farmer's bible."

"Again, sounds good to me."

Nguyen asked, "Since I have no family or any-where else to go — but I do know how to make things grow here — I don't need to leave. If that's all right?"

"It's completely up to you. Anyone who wants

to stay is welcome. We will be establishing our company headquarters here — and I believe we'll make the space station above into a shipyard. We have things to offer no other shipyard can equal. We may be on the edge of the galaxy, but we will put Homestead on the star charts. And that means there will be jobs."

Ash looked over the crowd for other questions. When there were none he asked, "Who sent out the message about the ambush in the Ranvone system?"

An attractive young woman held up her hand in the front edge of the crowd.

"Jaxlynn Shellanberger," she said. She had a heart-shaped face and thick copper colored hair.

"You are brilliant. Had it not been for you, we would not be here today."

"The pirates killed all my family the day they attacked our cruise ship. I have no home to go do. Would it be possible to join your crew?"

"Absolutely," Ash said. "How does the rank of ensign sound to you?"

"That's an officer, isn't it?"

"If you don't display what it takes to be an officer, I've never seen it."

"But I know nothing about being an officer."

"OJT, Ensign Shellanberger. You'll be on my

new ship and do just fine. Your new family will help you every step of the way."

"What's your new ship, Sir.

"It's going to be called 'The Lady In The Lake.'"

CHAPTER THIRTY-FIVE

Doc convened a meeting of the Round Table owners. There were four seats filled since Yardmaster Santana Vanderhoff's daughter, Lt. Commander Starla was joining them. The Yardmaster didn't understand what was happening.

He turned and spoke to Doc. "You called this meeting. What's it all about?"

"Number one," Doc said, "Santana, you've always worked for a corporation. We now own a planet and a space station. How about we build a shipyard there?"

"At the edge of the galaxy?"

"It would be your shipyard."

"That would be wonderful," Vanderhoff said, "but who would ever come out there?"

"Let's deal with the second item on our agenda. Ash?"

"I propose," the Admiral said, "we make Starla a full member of the company. All in favor signify by raising a hand."

Both Ash and Doc voted in favor. Starla glanced over at her father with a bemused look.

"Look," Santana said raising a bushy eyebrow, "of course I'm in favor — but from a business point of view what is her contribution to the company?:

"A patent she owns," Ash said.

"For advanced FTL drives," Doc picked up the thread. "There's also the one for cloaking — but that's not on our little round table at the moment. For the FTL idea she buys in fully. Ash and I agree — so even if you don't like it, the vote is two to one."

Santana raised his right hand. "Of course I agree. Why wouldn't I like it?" To his daughter he asked, "You are willing to part with a patent — and the income potential?"

"This one," she said. "However, only to our company — and if we use it out at the Homestead yard only?"

"Now that's an idea," Santana said. "That would make it worth the trip out there."

To all Starla said, "I still have some improvements in mind — but for our company ships only right now."

"And the cloaking?" Santana asked.

"I think we should keep that one within the company, Father, and the fleet — for the time being, anyway."

"Then," Doc suggested, "let's make this our plan. Move our HQ and all operations to Homestead. And build a shipyard on that space station. Which, by the way, needs a name."

"How about calling it simply, 'The Place.'"

No one got it.

"As in," Starla said, "A Clean Well-lighted Place.'"

"It's simple," Doc said.

"And easy to remember," Ash agreed.

"Why not?" Santana laughed. "The Place. That's what my father used to call his work whenever he'd go off to work."

"I remember," Starla said.

~

THAT AFTERNOON another meeting was held at Xanadu Transit in a rented conference room. Attending this gathering were all Round Table ship's Captains, and NCOICs.

When everyone was seated, Ash stood and addressed the group. "I want your feedback on this. I have a major cultural change to suggest to the way we work."

He looked around the room before he said, "We are not a traditional military. We've been operating like one. And we are requiring the same sacrifices any military always has. I propose we change things. You here have been very careful in the choice of your teams. Yet, officers and enlisted need more than food, living conditions and opportunities for education and advancement for those who want it. What we need are our families."

There were wrinkling of foreheads all around the room.

"We are moving the company out to Homestead and every member of our crews will get some land there. We will also service and repair our ships at the shipyard that we'll build at the space station there. By the way, — we're going to call the station,'The Place.'"

Ash allowed this to sink in before he went on.

"We'll even construct our new vessels at our new home port. I'd like to begin with a new version of the T-Rex. We have two of them — one with all circuits fried still waiting for us near Ranvone. And the other at Homestead. Of course, that second one has the hell beat out of it. But together I believe they will make a one very durable, reliable, and, I hope, family livable vessel. With the use of new AI's Lt. Commander Vanderhoff has told me about — we won't need the size crew the originals did — not just on a T-Rex but on our other ships as well. But I want us to be able to take families with us. The military had always left their family behind — I'd like to change that. I believe this will make our force stronger and better serve sailors and their families.

"This will require some rethinking on our parts — and another reason to ensure we protect our ships because there will be more on the line than just ourselves. But as we prepare to cross the galaxy and prep for another war — we should become a different kind of force."

Ash paused and scanned the gathering again.

"Tell me what you think."

No one said anything for a few moments. This was such a radical idea.

"If we can do it," Captain Olin said, "this could

be not just a revolutionary idea — but a new way of life."

"How about those who don't have a family?" NCOIC Deron Ficken asked.

"It's a possibility but not mandatory. I'd like to make it available," Ash said, "to those who qualify and are interested. I think some of our people will have to do some growing up and make their relationships more permanent. And I understand what it will do to the bunk buddy mentality. We can't command morality — but we all need to mature at some point in time."

The room was quiet again.

"Think this over," Ash challenged everyone. "We can meet again — as many times as needed. Those families who don't want to go with us when we deploy can stay at their home in Homestead. However, for those who want family with them — I would like to do that."

Ash paused and said, "The only order I'm giving is — go — think this over. We will have time as we move and build the new shipyard. If we can — let's make it work. Dismissed."

As Doc and Starla were leaving, he contacted her over her nerolink. "Alakazam. I think the magic door just opened."

Starla smiled and said to him, "I see the possibilities."

"And the Admiral does, too," Doc replied.

THE END

THANKS

Thank you for taking the time to read <u>A New War, THE ERRANT Vol. 1</u>. I hope you enjoyed it. If you did, please consider posting a short review on line at the site where you purchased the book and telling your friends. Word of mouth is an author's best friend and much appreciated. I love to write these stories, but it's even better to sell some and to know other people take some joy from them, too.

If you're interested in subscribing to my monthly newsletter, contact me at jacks@ wrightbridgepress.com. You will know when my next novel is coming out and a little bit about how I work. I would love to hear from you.

Thank you,
   Jack R. Stanley

[Murder in Muleshoe]
If you were murdered would they try to find the killer or plan him a parade?
[Guns Along The Rio]
In 1858, two fresh-off-the-ranch 17-year-olds join the Texas Rangers. What could possibly go wrong?
GO TO: eepurl.com/dKEi_Y

ABOUT THE AUTHOR

Jack R. Stanley is an award winning novelist, playwright, and screenwriter. As an officer and combat photographer in Vietnam, he earned the Bronze Star. Yet he says, "When you're in a fire-fight and everybody else on both sides have guns while you have a camera --- you get to change your pants a lot."

After his military service he received both his M.A. and his Ph.D. at the University of Michigan in Ann Arbor in Radio-TV-Film. His doctoral dissertation was on the long running TV series GUNSMOKE. Stanley also received two of Michigan¹s most prestigious creative writing awards, The Hopwood Award, one for a one-act play and the second for a novel.

Still married to his gifted high school sweet-heart, Stanley's first academic position was TV Area Head at The University of Texas at Austin's Department of Radio-TV-Film. He later moved to deep-south Texas and the Lower Rio Grande

Valley for a challenging position with The University of Texas-Pan American. Here he taught Theatre-TV-Film for 30 years in the Department of Communication serving as Department Chair at U.T.P.A. for 11 years. He did take one year out to work for The University of Alaska Anchorage as a visiting professor. Back in Texas, Stanley directed for stage at The University Theatre, produced and directed fifteen student staffed, cast, and crewed feature films, writing most of the original screenplays. Just a few of his credits are available on IMDB.com.

He now lives in the Texas Panhandle where he writes his fiction.

The Elected President

[Vietnam]
Through A Lens Darkly: Vietnam

[Mysteries]
Murder In Muleshoe
Corpse In Canyon
The Lovecraft Murders
Short Stories
TALES FROM THE ALASKAN GOLD RUSH
Klondike Justice
Dangerous Camp On The Kenai
The Winds of Skagway

Screenplays
6 and 10
The 7th Luger
Afternoon Delight
Angel's Revenge
Between Love And Murder
Blood Drive
Death Scene

The Defection of Grigori Dorsky

The Evil Eye

Fatty and Hearst

Gideon: The Horse That Saved Texas

Hell In Paradise

Hollowpoint

Holiday For An Assassin

Horse Thief Hollow

Incident A tLajitas

Love, Lust, & Life

Mom & Apple Pye

Pancho's Pilot

The Prometheus Peril

The Rape of Sarah Quinn

Reservations

River of Tears

Seven Reasons Why

The Thing About Love

The Texas Rattlesnake Murders

Too Good To Be True

The Vampire Rose

A Violent End

The Virgin Casanova

Plays

Antigone In Texas

Cyrano

The Last Virgin From Las Vegas

The Seven Keys

The Unwed Widow